CW00494384

Bristol Story Prize Anthology

Volume Fifteen

Bristol Short Story Prize Anthology Volume 15

First published 2022 by Tangent Books

Tangent Books, Unit 5.16 Paintworks
Bristol, BS4 3EH
0117 972 0645
www.tangentbooks.co.uk

Email: richard@tangentbooks.co.uk

ISBN: 9781914345241

Cover designed by Martyna Gradziel
www.martynagradziel.com

Layout designed by Dave Oakley, Arnos Design
www.arnosdesign.co.uk

Printed and bound by
CMP (UK)
G3 The Fulcrum
Poole, BH12 4NU

A CIP catalogue record for this book is available from the British Library
www.tangentbooks.co.uk
www.bristolprize.co.uk

Introduction

Thank you to everyone who entered the 2022 Bristol Short Story Prize. It's always thrilling to catch a glimpse of how much short story writing is happening around the world. Thanks to all of you for keeping the beautiful form of the short story in robust, dynamic and flourishing health.

The variety of themes and styles in this year's anthology provide a really expansive reading experience and showcase the flexibility and power of the short story. Huge congratulations to the 20 writers selected for the 15th BSSP collection; it is thrilling to be publishing your work.

Third prize goes to Johanna Spiers and her story, *OldFish*. Judge, Jessica Taylor, calls it "An arresting tale of grief and revenge, told in a language all too familiar to us today. This powerful story forces us to think about the lengths we will go to for justice."

Second prize is awarded to Sufiyaan Salam and his story, *Wimmy Road Boyz*. Tom Drake-Lee, one of this year's judging panel, says of Sufiyaan's story: "It fizzes with enormous energy to reveal the complex lives of friends as they wrestle with the nature of friendship, identity and culture. It is extraordinary. "

And this year's winning story is *A Cure for All Our Ills* by Diana

Powell. Judge, Irenosen Okojie, hails it as "A brilliant, hypnotic piece from an exciting voice. I had the feeling of holding my breath through this story. From its powerful, palpable opening, I was immediately invested. The use of tension, the exploration of religion, of a sacred space becoming dark and unknown propels this world forward. Every word on the page is earned."

Our readers and judges have made a huge contribution to this year's anthology and competition, and we are extremely grateful for their commitment to the reading and decision-making processes, and their role in the development of the Bristol Short Story Prize.

Thanks to Richard Jones and Tangent Books for guiding and nurturing the production of this anthology.

Many thanks, also, to Mimi Thebo, Billy Kahora and Harry Boucher at Bristol University for their support, and to Martin Booth and Bristol 24/7.

The arresting anthology cover has been designed by recent University of the West of England Illustration degree graduate, Martyna Gradziel. Thanks to Martyna, to course leaders Chris Hill and Jonathan Ward and the 3rd year students for this year's inspiring cover design project.

And a big thank you to you for buying our latest anthology. We hope the stories keep you riveted and spark your curiosity as much as they have us.

Joe Melia
BSSP Co-ordinator

1ˢᵗ Prize
Diana Powell

Diana Powell's stories have featured in a number of competitions, such as the 2020 Society of Authors ALCS Tom-Gallon Trust Award (runner-up), the 2020 TSS Cambridge Prize (3rd place) and the 2019 Chipping Norton Literature Festival Prize (winner). Her work has appeared in several anthologies and journals, including Best British Short Stories 2020 (Salt). Her novella, *Esther Bligh*, was published in June 2018 (Holland House Books). Her collection of stories, *Trouble Crossing the Bridge*, came out in 2020. Another novella, *The Sisters of Cynvael*, won the 2021 Cinnamon Press Literature Award and will be published next year.

A Cure For All Our Ills

They are taking us to the church again.

Our mothers, sisters, maids, leading us up the breathless holloways or along the ancient drove paths.

It is the same when they bring the animals, except *those* are tethered, nose or neck, with brass rings and leather halters. They don't do that to us. Not yet. No more than the grip of bony fingers beneath the elbow, a pinch, the press of ragged nails into our tender flesh, to guide us, now and then.

Today, there are two others approaching the crossroads.

That means there will be three of us today. There have been more in the past. Six, I remember, once. When a girl no longer appears, I like to think it is because she has 'improved'. There is no need for her to come any more. But it is not always so.

At the crossroads, we come together, shuffle our feet, bow our heads, then peek up through our hair. Perhaps we recognise each other from before, unless there is a new girl – as I was once, as we all were.

Most of us come from the farms. This is a farming county, in a farming country, after all. Wales. Perhaps there will be a cluster of houses. Or an occasional cottage. There are a few Big Houses – a rectory, a manor. But mostly farms.

Esther, who keeps her head lowest, is from a farm up and down the hill. The other, Lizzie, who was new last time, doesn't quite know where she comes from. And there is me, Sarah. I am one of those from a Big House. The one you might see, if you climbed to the top of the church tower, and looked west from there, towards the ocean. But they do not allow us to climb up the tower, nor any high place.

Sometimes we say hello. Sometimes we don't. Those who lead us may exchange a few words about the weather. The weather is important in a farming community.

We move on to the church together.

The church always looks lonely. It stands there, on its own, the nearest dwelling hidden behind the trees. It belongs to a saint no-one knows anything about, or why he should have a church here. Nothing like his/our Patron, with his Cathedral resting in the nearby vale, dedicated there, and in every parish. *This* saint went elsewhere quickly, it is said. Perhaps he was as lonely as his church.

It has a tall, thin tower, thinner than most. It is of dark stone, with gaps etched for windows. No bright patchwork glass here. No wash of slaking lime to cheer it.

Everything about it is dour.

We are not here for the church.

That is what people mistake.

Thinking we have come to have the Lord bless us, his saint bless us (whoever that saint is), thinking we have come here to pray for His Son's Saving. Because Jesus can do that.

No.

It is nothing like that.

We are led around the building, into the churchyard that circles around the church. A circular bound means something, the Wise Folk, the grandmothers and Dyn Hysbys say. It has something to do with beliefs far older than God, Christ, their saints, known or unknown. *That* is why we are here.

'Eat,' they say – our mothers, sisters, maids, whoever has brought us.

'Eat!'

The cattle have been here before us, we can see. No more than a few hours ago, the deep imprints of their hooves, churning the ground to mud, so there is meagre grass left. Among the mud, their ordure is mixed in. Their urine fills the clefts in the ground.

Esther begins to cry.

'Come on now, eat.' They wander away then. Perhaps they wish to talk more about the weather.

'Look, there,' I say, spying a patch beneath the hedge ignored or unnoticed by the cattle. 'Perhaps there...'

I am allowed to bring a blanket – I am from the Big House, after all. I spread it out, near the untouched spot, and the three of us sit down.

Anyone passing might think we are here for a picnic.

Three young ladies on an outing. Yes, they have chosen a rather strange spot, but, still...

Three young ladies making most of their leisure by eating out of doors.

And yes, they are about to eat something. Look!

But no, we are not here for a picnic.

I pluck a handful of the grass, wipe it on the leaves in the hedge, then give some to each of the girls.

Lizzie takes a blade between her thumb and forefinger, and touches it to her teeth. It is, after all, only her second visit. Her face is lost in gurns and ruffles.

Esther and I chew solidly, our eyes fixed on some distant place. We have found it the best way.

In the beginning, in the time the Wise Folk talk about, there was no need to eat the grass. A spring came out of the ground, in the middle of the circle. That was when they noticed it, they say. Perhaps it was just one cow first – a favourite milker drying up, attacking the hand that fed it. Or a dog. Perhaps it was a dog. A gentle beast, who started growling at its shadow and barking at the clock in the hall. And then... droplets of spit, seething at the mouth, so they knew, for sure. The Sickness. And perhaps this cow, or that dog, wandered into this field by chance, his master in pursuit, and stopped to drink at the spring, as if drawn to it, having refused all other water.

Perhaps the foaming stopped then, together with the strange behaviour, and the creature was cured. They tell.

And all other suffering animals were brought from round about, and they were cured, too.

So then the people were brought.

Perhaps.

Lizzie shucks the shred of grass from her lips, pulls a doll from the pocket of her apron. She holds it tight, and rocks it from side to side. They gave it to her when they took her baby from her, she told us, last time. The baby she wasn't supposed to have. 'You are too young to have babies,' her mother said. 'You are unwed,' her father shouted. The baby wasn't supposed to happen, yet it did. And then it wasn't there. She croons to the doll, instead.

I tell Lizzie about the spring, thinking to help her understand why she is here.

'But I do not have the Sickness,' she says.

Lizzie is right. True, bubbles of spit formed at her lips, as they took her baby away. And she screamed and tore at the flesh of those nearest her. And true, since then, she has spent most of her days sitting in the corner, rocking her doll. But no, she does not have the Sickness.

'After a while,' I continue, 'they built the church, and the well dried up. The Sickness returned, until another poor, stricken animal strayed into the churchyard, ate the grass and was cured. 'The power of the spring has found its way into the grass,' they proclaimed. The church claimed it most, requiring all those who ate the grass to make some payment for the honour. Hence, the hole in the wall for our pennies. 'A small price to pay to rid you of the Sickness!' they said.'

'But I do not have the Sickness, either,' says Esther.

Esther sees things. Strange beings floating in front of her. Or places where she would like to go – green meadows, a lake – until they disappear.

When this happens, she shakes, cannot talk, and does not want to eat. She cannot sleep.

All this is just before her Bleeding, until after it.

They have had a doctor to examine her beneath. Then another, looking deeper into her, prodding and poking. They have tried this potion and that liniment, '*down there*'. There is talk of Esther being sent away. Of being locked up. They lock her up, now. Those days before, during and after her Bleeding.

In between, they send her to eat the grass.

'Later, it is said they put the grass between slices of bread and butter. Thick slices of farmhouse bread, spread with rich yellow butter, straight from the dairy. And fresh, lush grass, washed and patted dry, laid neatly, so that it sunk into the golden cream, lost there. There was a name for it, even. A Welsh name, being in Wales. *Porfar cynddeiriog.* As if it were special.'

Yes, indeed, in those days, it would most certainly appear that we were on a picnic, with our neatly cut sandwiches spread on our blanket, ready to eat.

'But they grew tired of this over time. Or forgot it. Just as they forgot the grass was for the Sickness – forgot, even, the Sickness, except for the farmers, wanting succour for their cows. 'Why not try it for other ailments?' someone said. 'These strange ailments suffered by young women, that there are no cures for. Why not just bring them here, and tell them to eat?' So they did.'

It was my governess who told me all this. I come from the Big House, after all. Rich enough to have a governess to teach me my lessons. Miss Marchant. Catherine. She told me all this as she was packing her bags; she, trying to explain to me, as I explain to Lizzie.

Grass meant something other, before Cat left. Grass was for lying in, beside her, after we had swum in the lake. We laughed at our naked bodies streaked green. She licked my stained skin, then we swam again. The water washed over us. 'We are pure,' we thought.

'Dirty, filthy. The sin of the Devil. Unholy.' – these were the words they used for her.

I, the child, was ill or sick. They brought me here, straight away. 'Eat,' they said.

'Neither do I have the Sickness,' I say.

Esther is beginning to retch.

This is something that happens. It is what happens with dogs, after all – they, choosing to eat the grass when they need to rid something noxious from their innards. Is this what our guardians think? That we will retch up our ailments? Or our sins? That they are sins? That the demons, devils – whatever is inside our hearts, minds, stomachs – will rise up through our mouths?

They – those who have brought us today – have wandered out of sight, searching for somewhere to chew cud of their own, it might be said.

'Come,' I say, to Esther and Lizzie. We get up. I take their hands. 'Let us go into the church, and climb up the tower. It would be nice to see the world from there.'

And yes, it is nice, when we reach the top, and look out across the land, the wind blowing through our hair.

And yes, as I thought, if we look past the fields, across to the dell where the Patron Saint's cathedral is cradled, we can see a circle of blue, caught between the trees. The lake. A bird's flight away.

Below, those who brought us – our mothers, sisters, maids – have realised our absence, and come to look for us, and spotted us up here.

They are waving to us, shouting. 'Come down,' they say.

We wave back.

'What shall we do?' I ask Esther and Lizzie. 'Shall we go back down, or wander further?'

'Down' is the muddy grass where the cattle trample, sending the gravestones upwards, at strange angles. Coffins have been pushed to the surface in wet winters, the wind has splintered the wood, the corpses within seeping into the earth. And there is the venting of the beasts. And there is so little grass left now, besides. What kind of cure could it give?

Ahead, is the emerald green sward, with the lake beyond. Blue sky, green, green, grass, lapping water, all so beautiful and pure.

Which shall we choose?

We take each other's hands, and step forward.

***

We are going to the church again, today.

We walk arm in arm, up the holloway and along the drove path, chatting, laughing, the three of us. Esther, Lizzie and me.

At the crossroads, we meet Lucy, Mari, Mary and Bet – the girls I remember from before. We greet each other, then go on, waving at another group, who are wending across the fields.

Yes, a dozen young ladies in all. Anyone seeing us might think we are out for a ramble in the countryside, or a 'rendezvous' for conversation and merriment. A 'divertissement' such as young ladies enjoy!

But no, that is not why we are here.

We move into the circle of the churchyard together.

Now, we must stop our chatter, and turn our upward mouths down, gritting our faces into pictures of sadness, while we gather around the open grave, waiting for its coming incumbent.

That is why we are here.

The Sickness returned in the summer, the worst it had ever been, afflicting our mothers, sisters, maids; our fathers, brothers, labourers, taking so many from us, from our small farming community. *This* burial is the latest of many, with the graves butting against each other, filling every last corner of the cemetery, pushing up more of the grass than any of the beasts' hoof-prints, destroying any left-over growth more fully than the ordure and urine, the rotting corpses, the winter weather.

Only the few farmers who recalled the words of the Wise Folk stay well. And us. The girls who had been made to eat the grass, as a cure for all our unfathomable ills. We, too, remain unscathed.

So we come to mourn each death, being the only ones fit and able to do so, and pray to the saint (whoever he may be) and his Patron, and our Lord and His Son; pray that the dead's souls go to the place they deserve (wherever that place may be). And thank Them, too, quietly, under our breath, for what we have received.

2nd Prize
Sufiyaan Salam

Sufiyaan Salam was born in Blackburn, and is now based in Manchester, UK. He currently works as a script editor for BBC Studio's JoJo & Gran Gran, and was a part of the BBC Writersroom Northern Voices group in 2022. Outside of the 9-5, he keeps himself busy with various prose, television and theatre projects in development. His short story, *The Kashmiri and the Romanian*, was published by Bandit Fiction in 2020.

Wimmy Road Boyz

C old rain falls down on Manchester as the boys head towards...

***

1: THE CURRY MILE TO HELL

"WIMMY ROAD BRO! WIMMMY ROOOOAD!"

upfront shouting, IMMY, o.g bradford bad bwoy, onehandedly cruising and bruising in a white beemer – a real powerbox, yaar! – booming bare bhangra bangers bruv–

moving as a massive, well sticky traffic, veering samosa-closer towards wilmslow road, the curry mile, g! that neon-scented mecca, a jannat-ul-firdous of kebab houses, burger joints, shisha bars and–

"oi, we're almost there now, let's put some real music on, my guy."

KHAN, cushy in the backseat, this brother an up-and-coming rapper, bars about bandos and badness betrayed by the cushy middle-class shadow under which he so shamefully sprouted.

"it strikes me that the beginning of the night is always so broad-stroked, the possibilities almost infinite. and as the seconds go by – as we near our destination, our time is spent and we are set in stone. the more we live, the less we are free."

HARIS, staring out the window, philosophy subreddits doing bares, spitting knowledge to mask crippling ptsd owed to time spent in various actual bandos and betrayals beyond. a dangerous guy, read rushdie in juvie.

the beemer skrrt-skrrts to a slowdown, red light ones–

KHAN takes out a spliff–

IMMY's like yo, don't stink up the car man, my mums gets bare suspicious about it recently, asking me shit like what's that weird curry smell, mandem, i think she *suspects*, ya get me?–

then HARIS is all like did you know the first drug baron in the uk was some indian dude called the doctor, he was a laser scientist and also had pakistani slaves, this is the real british history they don't be teaching us in schools –

to which IMMY and KHAN both let out an exasperated *aur* thinking oi oi *oi* i hope we're there soon innit–

meanwhile oblivious to their scorning, HARIS tackles a Rubik's Cube missing yellows and oranges, spinning and clicking through oriental possibilities like some great god above–

***

2: WE BE PROMMING ALL NIGHT BITCH, SAARI RAAT

Woohoo! Imran's mother's lipstick adorns his cheek. Her hands look like this [coarse and veiny like a Snicker's bar left out in the sand, the result of minimum-waging it for fifteen years straight] so his can look like this [holding up his Maths GCSE certificate, finally passed on the third attempt, masha-allah!]. The whole day a blur: a meal with the family, cash in hand from his cooing aunties, a cheeky text to the lads' groupchat:

'Aur, boys. Let's redo Prom.'

The memory of Prom drips like warm condensation from those times – four or five years ago, the so-called glory days. They'd turned up in a Bentley paid for by Imran's dad and driven by Haris's, each experiencing major life developments over the course of the night…

Immy smoked weed for the first time. M*mmm*!

Haris made out with a white girl for the first time. M*mmmmmmm*!

Khan got kicked out his family home for two weeks straight after writing his father a letter renouncing his belief in Allah. He was later allowed back into the family home only after an exorcism was performed on him which did, in all fairness, cure him of said atheism, though it did also push him into the trapping lifestyle, eventually leading to his incarceration and subsequent PTSD...

–Mm.

But! Before Khan's dad's life and pride collapsed and after the sweaty dancing and muffled smoking, the boys had hopped into the back of the limo and spent the night downing cans of cider whilst the chauffeur (some hearing-aid uncle paid to keep schtum) drove them to and around curry mile, up and down, over and over and over and over and over and over and over and over and over and over and–

<vomit-sounds>

***

3: RIDE IT, COME TOUCH MY SOUL

down the winding, binding road they whistled, winked and whooped, vimmmy road brooo, vimmmy road–

KHAN steps on it, always been a bit of a paul walker type, if one day the speed kills me and that–

"yo, not gonna lie, them movies went kinda downhill after he died," IMMY, something of a movie buff, ticking off the imdb top 250 when mandem around him were flicking off clitorises, "them movies don't respect aristotelian narrative–"

KHAN tuts. "bro, you film nuts always tryna ruin good honest entertainment, innit? real pakis don't give a fuck about no aristotle, g! they went to space in the last movie. in a car. how you gon' be mad at that?"

"you boys ever notice there's no muslims in those films?" HARIS, woke for brownie points, plays twitter like its tetris, "riz ahmed says muslims being excluded from hollywood films directly leads to violence perpetuated against muslims."

yawn yawn yawn.

HARIS takes his eyes off the road to face the others. "yo, what's rule one of travelling in the knight rider with me, boys? heh?"

"no victimisation," they mutter boyscoutishly, "no feeling sorry for ourselves."

"that's it, boys! now, say it with me, where we at–?"

WIMMY ROAD, WIMMY ROAD, WIMMY ROOOOAD–

***

4: ASIAN PROVOCATEUR

Now, I was at the Curry Mile yesterday with two of my mates, they're here tonight – that's Imran and there's Khan, give 'em a round of applause. Yay!

The Curry Mile, for those who don't know, it's not, it isn't an actual mile made of actual curry, you know what I mean? Easy mistake to make! I remember I told Khan, like 'oh, I'm going to travel down Curry Mile today' and he thought I meant – and this is true! – he genuinely thought I was about to put on a bib and swim mouth agog into 528 feet of boiling lamb bhuna. And I had to say, I had to make very, very clear: the Curry Mile is not an actual mile made of actual curry!

But what *is* the Curry Mile then, if not an actual mile made of actual curry? Well, the Curry Mile is, in fact, just part of the much bigger Wilmslow Road, about half a mile long, home to at least 70 different South Asian and Middle Eastern establishments. So, it's not an actual mile made of actual curry, but is, rather disappointingly, just a half-mile made of tarmac and tax evasion. Right?

And I'll give you a fun fact, okay? – Wilmslow Road has the word 'slow' in it. Which, and I'll tell you, that's preeeetty ironic given how many drivers have been killed speeding along it, but that's a story for another day…

***

5: MUNDIAN TO BACH KE

riding jayseanishly, doing up curry mile, the sa-vift sa-mell of samosay

26

sa-zizzling in the air–

HARIS stares out as a zodiac of neon bleeds into the beemer's windscreen and – looking into the rearview mirror – he notices the chromatically abberated patterns dancing on the soft skin of the men sitting in the back seat–

IMMY's hand numb, like a statue. placed awkwardly on the ass of the middle seat some twenty minutes ago, when the uber first melded with city centre traffic–

KHAN had clocked straight away, of course. but the uncle up front is an apna, creepily side-eyeing like some beedy, pervert lizard. real talk, making KHAN itch like paki bacteria under microscope–

as the audi shudders finally past whitworth park, standing only four cars from the start of curry mile, IMMY inches his hand along – why not, so what? – brushing KHAN's butter-soft thigh–

KHAN seizes up, heart thumping like a dhol. they had done up canal street. done up deansgate. even done up bollywood at printworks odeon... but outside the steamed-up windows shone the dazzling holi vision of a homeland that shifted too easily between good cop/bad cop. paralysed like michelangelo's david, uncle up front still staring – was this geezer not ashamed, fam? – KHAN felt trapped in amber knowing the only remedy – the warm delight found in his lover's embrace – was simultaneously the source of his great discomfort...

meanwhile upfront, crawling snailishly ahead – this phenchode traffic! – HARIS continues to watch the petrol-spill ballet on the men's cheeks

– who after first saying salaam when they got in had retreated into a spiky silence, cowering in opposite corners of his prius.

"so... what your plans are for the night?"

IMMY and KHAN glance at each other, a bucket of heat spilling over them.

"halal stag do, uncle." IMMY mumbles. "my boy's getting hitched."

"ohhh! mubarak!" HARIS wants to slam down the horn, PEEP PEEP PEEEEEP, rare to hear such news in these haram times... but he picks up the sting in the air.

"may i please ask, love marriage or arranged?"

KHAN pulls his hand back. IMMY notices. shifts.

"arranged."

"ah. very good. means more mystery for you later. you see these english, they find out everything about the girl for years and years and *then* they marry? but much of the magic is in slowly peeling back layers. arranged prevents all problems!"

and then, and here's the thing, KHAN doesn't know why he says it, but he does: "well, actually uncle... to be real, like... there's someone else. is the problem."

HARIS turns. notices the boys properly for the first time. tries to recall what love had felt like at that age. all-consuming and red, like a rash. a freefall off the edge into hot-hell. lust as compelling despite the overwhelming stench of sin.

"actually… i also knew another." HARIS looks away now. "before marriage. someone else i cared for. back in pakistan."

"what happened?"

the car in front moves up. beeping from behind. IMMY and KHAN's fingers find each other. interlock. tears in their eyes now, all of them.

the outside lights performing reddish rain.

***

6: GROUP OF THREE BOYS BY AMRITA SHER-GIL

Traffic long, not limber, rain, thunder all asunder,
Curry Mile, worry denial, blurry smile,
Travelling far, three boys in car, long way away in dark–

Haris sculpts Indian ink passers-by into his sketchbook, resting on edge of the car door. His silky linework waves vibrationally, reflecting rain-mottled windows. Beside him, Imran stares in delight, a sparkling hunger in his eyes. Up front, Khan taps his fingers to luminescent music in his head, enamoured by the refracted neon puddles in his eyeline.

"Say, boys," Haris begins, putting his brush down, "who would you say is the best Manchester painter right now?"

"Hmm," Imran hums, leaning back, "well, she's young, but I really like Louise Giovanelli. I think, given how obsessed with imagery our society is, you know, mythmaking via imagery, she's a super fascinating figure because she's kind of interrogating the way we see."

"Oh yes, haan-ji," Khan nods like an excited puppy, "I saw some of her works at the Grundy. She's great. She did all them curtains and things, innit?"

"Yep, that's her. She's sick!"

"I don't know her work, give me a minute…" Haris pulls out his phone and the boys gather around Louise Giovanelli's Instagram portfolio like it's a campfire, scrolling through and looking in awe at her body of work. Soaking in the flavours.

Imran looks back at Haris. "What do you think, my guy?"

"I think it goes deeper than interrogating the way we see. It feels kinda like, I don't know – she's a youngish artist trying something new, but this feels like it exists in history, right? Like, her work knows its place in the canon and is actively challenging and embracing that. And looking away. All at the same time. It's like when Busta Rhymes sampled the Knight Rider theme song for 'Fire it Up' and then Panjabi MC sampled 'Fire it Up' to make 'Mundian To Bach Ke' and then Jay Z jumped on a remix called 'Beware of the Boys". It's reappropriating history. Making something new with it."

"For sure. It's all very pointedly fragmented. So… of its time."

"Right? Fragmented like this jagged air we're all breathing. Right now, all identity is mutating. How we see ourselves, our personal histories. The self-editing, multi-sampling, ridiculously media-literate generation. Distilling an entire culture and history into these little moments we can latch onto as we're swept away in the tide. It's post-context. The TikTok-ification of time itself."

"Kya baat hai, yaar! A glorious manifesto for the future of art!"

"And most importantly," Khan grins, "the pictures are pretty to look at."

The moment carries in the air for a few seconds. The boys reflect. Traffic shuffles on, inch by inch by inch. Outside, children chirp, couples coo, cars chrrrrrh–

Khan stares out the window as the car moves again. One question in his mind: how would Louise Giovanelli paint *this* scene, right now? Curling over to a new page in his sketchbook, he begins to slowly find the soft contours of his answer:

Moments shrivel into minutes,
sketches pirouette into drafts,

redrafts.
Night hangs in the air like
a soft coat, so
patient, so wistful.

Night falls,
rain calls,
wind blows.

Women whistle,
men diddle,
children giggle.

Cars huff,
smokers puff,
students cuff.

The making of an image unmade,
the translation of a Rubik's Cube shattering
in time, not remembered any other way.

Life,
preserved and denied in the same breath.
Identity, minus internal consistency.

In other words:
Poetry.

***

7: EVERYBODY NEEDS A BOSOM FOR A PILLOW

"listen, let's just enjoy tonight boys. that's it."

IMMY, calm and collected, smirking up rusholme in the freshest fit, curry mile and that, driving jaldi-jaldi in a pearlescent paki-mobile–

wimmy road, where da wimmin are wibble-wobble wildin bro, wiiiiimmmy rooooooooad–

past jilanis
past sadaf
past dubai cafe

bare homeless open-palming for tea and biccies
bare families on the hunt for motherland scran
bare pigs on horses when nobody even doing nuttin–

"oi! we're down to the last bottle!" HARIS, agitated, shaking the nos canister to confirm. how they got through that much already, yo?

KHAN, wacked out, drools gothic spittal from a rapidly expanding-deflating red balloon, absent-mindedly giving it updownupdown, repeat repeat repeat–

"this gets the lines in my head proper spicy, you know them ones? motherfucker, these balloons got me riding up the scoville scale, ya get me?"

ugh. barely 9pm, sun's down, jinns out, shits drying out. all JD up front but no cups to mix with pepsi max cherry. fuck-a-sake, brooo.

but look outside, g. bare gyally on scene, i'm tellin ya!

"i'm tryna get kuri tonight, me. a fat arse, mate–"

wolfishly, KHAN slams down the horn, giving it PEEP PEEP PEEEEP at a group of shining hourglass figurines–

"–a-wooooooooooooooh!"

HARIS scoffs, all wifed up, so nights like these are no stakes, just vibes. he taps IMMY's chest, giving it, "this guy's a joker, fam. he can't get no girls."

"hey! i get bare girls, me! literally was just texting gyally then, my g, this bird is beggin' for it too, wallahi bro, watch me get it licked tonight–"

the shaking of heads. "this guy, bruv. ehvy, you was texting no-one, say allah-ni-kasam–"

IMMY's getting bare upset now. slamming on the brakes. like a whoopy cushion, this boy 'bout to burst!

"yarrah, boys, this ain't some street shit what he done to me, you know that–?"

HARIS's eyeballs full of blood facing IMMY and KHAN fully square in the rear-view mirror. oi oi *oi*, this guy might be serious you know—

some janglee screams outside, pay no mind.

"what's up g, you can talk to me about anything, you know, day or night?"

wharra relief. okay strap in, lads—

HARIS breathes deep. the car some four-wheeler safe space. the two of them cacooned by their long-enduring friendship – a ten-year run founded on mutual appreciation of whiskey, weed and women – but they'd never chatted much deeper than, say, israel/palestine or the economic implications of blackburn rover's exit from the premier league – and it was never nuttin personal besides—

"it hurts, man. what he did. this ain't street beef, you get me? like... i'm literally, i'll be real, i'm in therapy for this. genuine person-centred trauma therapy, like, an 8-week course on nhs, right now, this ain't no joke, you get me. and it hurts to feel like a victim bro, but after what harry did to me, that's all i fucking am and it's ripping me apart man. like i feel like a fucking – even just driving down this road is taking me back, my heart beating like some shaadi dhol, i feel like, flipping, you know britney spears shaving her head, proper like mental breakdown vibes bro—"

the cacophony of the curry mile fades away. silence in the beemer.

"–he's ripped my whole life apart and i don't know how i'm going to get back from it, move on, be normal again, that make sense? i just wanna enjoy shit but there's nutting there to enjoy, you get me, my whole history has been corrupted, i got bare poison burning up my bloodstream my g, i feel like toilet paper flushed away, all clogged up, you get me?"

and KHAN did get him, in a way, because wasn't life that exactly–

fucking hand in blender type shit
underwater scream type shit
scratching off ya brain type shit
nails digging deep type shit

and fleeting images of all the girls from clubs he'd danced so happily with – antwerp 2016, if you know you know – the half-italian-half-papau new guinean dancer he'd met, with wildly electric hair, who grabbed his hands so tightly, whose best friend pinched his cheek to call him cute, who said she approved – and they had danced and they had bitten each other's lips – whilst his boys looked on, clicking fingers, so proud, so free – and then she led him to the smoking area where they talked for what seemed like hours – and i don't mean about the weather, i mean deep shit – she was with her white friends tonight, said the way men were treating her versus them was hardly surprising yet staggering at the same time – *you gotta laugh!* – he mentioned the way he and the boys hadn't been let into most of the clubs they tried to get into, how even *this* place had required a 5 min conviction speech before the bored bouncer sighed fuck it and let them in – *if you don't laugh, you'll only cry!* – how jarring life gets, how boring it is, how tiring – their hands wound together so tightly it hurt – the party illuminating in her eyes, so wide, so fucking free–

and then she'd gone to the bathroom with her friends, and then her and her friends – out on a hen do, as it turns out – had left without saying goodbye – he watched them go, heart sinking – was it something he said, had she hated the time they'd shared – too paralysed to run after her, get her number, see if there wasn't something there, he instead turned his back, stomach numb – spotting the next girl, some breathtakingly beautiful blondie with nails white enough to distract from the pain – and they talked for a while and he bought her a drink and maybe something cudda happened – but the conversation fell flat and besides, it was all numb down there by now anyway–

and he never got her name, the italian-papau new guinean dancer with the wild hair – that's probably why he's telling this story right now, to grab her attention, before sunrising the ting – cos he knew so much about her life, all the ungoogleable desires and depressions – he knew her taste and touch, scratches from her nails scored deep like victory markers – but not her name – nothing useful, nothing to suggest a future for them both–

***

8: BIG TROUBLE DOWN IN LITTLE ASIA

i wanna write some poetry that goes right up above
tryna get so i can bash a paki with some love

mensturating paki got that tiber kind of flow
pussy freshly skinhead got that st george kinda glow

altab ali dying whilst those whiteys on the moon
baby enoch on my door so i can powell you so soon

im tryna fly my plane between them twins you got up there
treat me like an airport come and strip me with no care

im tryna bash my pakis like im tryna bash my meat
make a curry mile of self-loving where all of us can eat

***

9: DON'T FORGET ABOUT THE DEEN, SEERAT AL-MUSTAQEEM

so deep into his own blighted memory did the driver, KHAN, forget to—

many, many KHANs out there bro, we sure it's him?—

thinking back to how sick that prom was, his first kiss—

no, that's IMMY, i think?—

the apostasy letter, losing religion was like losing all foundation, every truth he'd ever known ripped to shit, and then when the kala-jadoo-saab, i don't know his name the shady fucker, had him in that dark room, pushing him here and there, ripping the jinn from within his tinted chest–

wait, no, who's the other one again? HARIS, yeah, yeah, wait, was it him?–

his mum who had worked so hard for him to just fuck around, a car so polished and fresh, spinning wondrous donuts in the carpark after dark, like his mum ain't fully in debt for him over it, like they ain't all skimping on groceries to keep up payments, like he ain't just some little entitled prince stocking up on shit skunk and paranoia, feet up whilst his sisters juggle coursework and house chores and–

yo, but what about–?

who says IMMY ain't real man, who says paki rappers cant do nuttin, and university education means fuck all, money ain't that much of an escape, KHAN the khan, stripped of his royal title, a boy born the day the planes hit the towers, aged six when airport staff first asked him if he was personally involved in the london bombings, aged 16 when he first scoffed at a passer-by paki walking hand-in-hand with some gori larki, thinking yo, white girl like that, this geezer must be grooming her fam, before immediately throwing up at the idea that every phenchode pair of eyes to ever lay on him his whole life must be thinking that same sick, automatic shit–

thinking therapy was gonna be like the sopranos but it was more like the shower scene in psycho–

eeek! eeek! eeek!
telling his therapist, like, yo, racism kinda fucked me up, i'm like super
embarrassed at how much that shit makes me crumple–

telling his therapist, like, yo, i'm deep-down looking in the mirror like
i'm dracula bruv, making eye contact with my reflection and not seeing
nuttin' there–

telling his therapist, like, yo, you're the only motherfucker in my
life showing me love but i still ain't telling you shit about my self-
extinguishing ideations, mr. just so you know if i ever suspect you
might be at risk of hurting yourself, it's my honour-bound duty to–

shut the fuck up–

i'm a phenchode flesh and blood animal, g!

on gang, let me speed-run this motherfucker bro, giving it one last
jummah namaaz, kneeling down on fire and broken glass, asking for
forgiveness, past and future–

doing it like, yo, keep my family safe allah-paak
give them happiness, give them peace
not just my household but everyone
the palestinians, the uyghurs, the people in yemen and syria
flipping everyone man!
i want everyone happy and at peace–

hard to tell if them bottles were open before it happened hard to tell if it

were a slip of the road hard to tell if they weren't trying to cause terror–
cuh you know what the daily mail's gon' say, innit?

KHAN's grip kinda fading, steering wheel kinda on its ones now–

HARIS's eyelids shutting, outside sounds some fleeting discord–

IMMY giving it like, keep me in your duas guys, i'm 'bout to push
down real blind–

cuh they taking they hands off now–

corner of some long-abandoned pub. boarded up and shit. no
pedestrians, no worries–

three boys giving it: allah forgive us, for our mouths are all out of
screams–

***

It was raining in Manchester. Three Asian boys were killed in a car
accident, driving down Curry Mile. That's all we know so far. That's all
the facts we have.

3rd Prize
Johanna Spiers

Johanna Spiers is a qualitative health researcher by day and a writer by night. She is currently querying agents with her novel, *Social Death*, in which a snarky barmaid's ex declares her dead online – and is now coming for her IRL. Johanna also writes short stories about horrible people doing horrible things and, if you ask her nicely, the occasional funny poem. She DJs hip hop whenever she is allowed and believes yoga is the solution to most problems. Twitter (@JohannaSpiers) and Facebook (Johanna Spiers writer)

OldFish

Lolz01: OMG she said what??
Lolz01: did u tell Benson?

TayTay: nah angela would say i grassed and then theyd all hate me

Lolz01: U don't deserve this

TayTay: thanks you da best
TayTay: i wish u came 2 my school

Lolz01: me 2

TayTay: I did have one idea about angela tho

...

Lolz01: Yeah?

...

Lolz01: Tell me!

...

The three grey dots jumped up and down, mimicking Maureen's heart as she waited for Taylor to finish the story. Her carriage clock ticked out of time with those dancing dots.

Lolz01: TayTay? U still there hon?

The dots disappeared. Taylor had gone offline.

"Blast," said Maureen. She stood, that spot in her upper right thigh complaining, as it always did these days when she struggled to her feet. Might as well make a cuppa; Maureen knew from experience that she could be waiting a while now.

What did Taylor do when she vanished like this? Maureen never asked. Rather, she had learned to imitate these sudden, lengthy disappearances, vanishing from time to time and swooping back in when she could stand the silence no longer, all the while affecting unconcern. It was just how communication worked between young people these days, she understood that. She had listened to a Radio4 programme about the impact of social media on attention spans, so she knew all about it. Maureen knew that nothing aged a person like saying that things hadn't been this bad in their day, but heavens...

Putting her tea down, Maureen shut the laptop. A watched WhatsApp never pings, that was one of the things she'd learned since she had invented Lolz01 three weeks ago.

What to do while she waited? She could start dinner – but it was only 5.15pm. She could go to the library – but she hadn't finished her books yet. She could go to the tennis club – but she hadn't played tennis in 18 months now. She didn't suppose she would ever pick up her racket again.

Instead, she put on a podcast and dusted the pictures of her husband and granddaughter that hung on the sitting room walls.

***

Maureen had never heard the term catfish until her friend Gillian had told her about a podcast she had listened to. Well, to be honest, she had had to ask Gillian to explain what exactly a podcast was before they even got onto the catfish part. "I'm listening to a great podcast about catfishing," Gillian said, and Maureen wondered if the battery in her hearing aid needed replacing. Catfish. It sounded glamorous, sleek, quick. A cat who could glide through the water, turning on a tuppence. A fish that was beautiful, that eluded the shoal. A creature that made its own rules.

***

Taking her cup of tea, Maureen dozed in front of Pointless until that magical ping jolted her awake.

TayTay: soz mum was yelling about homework

TayTay: FFS she has no clue

Lolz01: Mine's the same, nightmare
Lolz01: What were you gonna say?

Taylor typed. The dots danced. Maureen looked at the photo of Laura she kept on her desk.

TayTay: I thought maybe if I could get angela on her own
TayTay: have proper chats
TayTay: maybe I could get her to see how shes making me feel
TayTay: what do u think?

What did she think about Taylor and her oppressor sitting down for a cosy chat over a can of Coke? Had Taylor forgotten that Angela had stolen her clothes from her locker, got her class to blank her for two entire days, got her into trouble with her English teacher? What did Maureen think? She thought that these bullies had to pay. Otherwise, they never stopped.

***

When Laura was a little girl, the air around her was always full of chatter, abuzz with books, golden with giggling. She told Maureen every grave detail of playground politics, sitting on Peter's lap, flinging her arms around both of them at every opportunity. Laura always sought out the children who had been cast aside, involving them in her games. That was who she was. Maureen knew she was hopelessly biased, but she had a sneaking suspicion that Laura might actually be perfect. In those early days, there had been no indication that anyone else felt differently.

***

Lolz01: yeah you could try that
Lolz01: But like...

...

Now Maureen was the one to trail off, leaving those dots dancing. She looked at Taylor's onscreen picture. A little bit plump, a little bit pretty, a little bit mousy. A little bit a lot of things. Still, Maureen longed to put an arm around her, tell her it would all be OK. Instead, she looked at the picture of Laura. Shining dark hair, warm eyes, kind smile. Yes, Maureen thought. She wasn't biased. Laura really was perfect.

Lolz01: u no angela's not a nice person
Lolz01: u need to fight fire with fire

The dots danced.

TayTay: OK
TayTay: wot do u think i should do?

***

The true crime podcasts were the ones Maureen enjoyed best, but she listened to others too. There were podcasts about everything you could think of. Cancer and comedy, politics and the paranormal. She had listened to a whole series about the effects of all the party drugs young people were taking these days. Podcasts were like the radio, but you could choose your own presenter and pause whenever you liked. They kept you company, chasing out the silence, filling the house with voices and facts and intrigue. She couldn't think what she had done without them.

***

Lolz01: Didn't u say your brother could get onto the dark web?

Maureen had heard about the dark web on a podcast. She'd Googled it and learned it was an eBay for sex, guns and substances. Maureen loved eBay, she used it to buy cheap wool and secondhand crime novels. It was ever so handy that Taylor's brother could access this dark version.

TayTay: yeah why?

Lolz01: Can u ask him to buy u some Es? Would he tell ur olds?

TayTay: Es???

Lolz01: yeah, u no, ecstasy tablets

TayTay: ROFL are u like 100 years old? u mean molly?

Blast. Molly, of course that was the term she should have used. Ecstasy was what Inspector Morse called it, not what teenagers today would say. With hands that were shaking even more than usual, she typed a reply.

Lolz01: Ha ha, I know, blame my bro, he's well old, that's what he calls it

TayTay: u got an older brother?
TayTay: pics????

Oh goodness, no. Now she'd have to invent a brother. It was more complex than you'd think, this catfishing lark. The conversation must be kept on track. Think, Maureen.

Lolz01: Trust, u don't wanna go there
Lolz01: But if I send u cash could ur brother get you some molly?

TayTay: probs he can get basically anything hes always bragging about it

Ok, good; they were back on track.

TayTay: but srsly WTF how is getting wasted gonna help??

Lolz01: Well…

***

It had all changed after Peter died. Laura came home from school quiet, her smiles made of cardboard. Shut herself in her room. Maureen tried to get her to talk, but Laura's face was as closed as her bedroom door. Teachers called her quiet, withdrawn. No friends came over. Laura would claim to be sick and Maureen, unsure what to do, thinking she must be missing her granddad, would feel her forehead and say she was fine, she had to go to school.

***

TayTay: god u think of the maddest things
TayTay: i wish u came 2 my school

Lolz01: me 2

TayTay: do u think u could move for year 12?
TayTay: we always get loads of new kids then

Lolz01: dunno. Maybe. I could ask my mum and dad I guess.

TayTay: OMG that would be so cool!!!!!!

Of course Maureen knew she couldn't go to Taylor's school. But she could invent an excuse later. It couldn't hurt to give the girl some hope, surely?

***

When Laura had shut herself in her room for the fourth night in a row without eating dinner, Maureen had knocked and gone in. Laura lay on the bed, her body small and still. Maureen sat next to her, stroked her hair. She tried to ask questions, but Laura stayed silent, so in the end, she just sat with her in the slowly darkening room, ignoring the twin rumbles of their stomachs, her hand on Laura's shoulder.

Finally, Laura spoke. Told Maureen about the used tampons they threw at her in the changing rooms, the bag of dog do they left in her desk, the digitally manipulated naked photographs they had sent round.

Laura told Maureen all these things, but she was too scared to tell her any names. To this day, Maureen still did not who her granddaughter's torturers were. When she'd gone to that whey-faced Mrs Godfrey and demanded to know who it was that was ruining Laura's life, the headmistress had claimed ignorance.

"I'll look into it," she had said, indicating a faded anti-bullying poster on the wall behind her. "We take this kind of thing seriously at Brickhill." But the woman was clearly so overwhelmed, so overworked that Maureen knew nothing would be done. This woman wasn't going to do anything to protect Laura.

Maureen left with no names and with helplessness heavy on her shoulders. She had never missed Peter more.

***

In reality, Maureen was neither a sleek black cat nor a shimmering goldfish. She was an old fish now, if she was anything at all. She was creaky, and slow, and weary. Her fingers ached in the rain, her eyes ached in the sun. But behind her keyboard, none of that mattered.

Maureen understood that behind your keyboard you could, if you wanted, pull on a shimmering costume and use it to transform yourself. No-one could stop you. You could become a magical creature, glancing and darting from conversation to conversation, being needed, being loved. The accepted wisdom was that the catfish were deceiving other people, taking them along for a ride. But Maureen knew that when you became a catfish, you were fooling yourself so fully that the old you – the you whose hips hurt and whose husband was long gone and who didn't push the headmistress hard enough on why your granddaughter had been replaced by a wraith – could be cast aside.

You could become someone powerful, someone with purpose. Someone perfect.

***

Lolz01: Did he get it?

TayTay: yeah. he said it was like 12 grams

Maureen sipped her tea and smiled at Laura's photograph. Did her smile deepen, just a little? Of course not, that was just Maureen's imagination. But if that was where her imagination wanted to take her, she wasn't going to say no.

TayTay: i dont know how much a person needs
TayTay: he gave me loads of shit about it but then got it for me anyway
TayTay: course the coin from u helped
TayTay: hes such a hypocrite just like everyone else

Maureen knew how much a person needed. That podcast had taught her that no single person needed 12 grams of MDMA, especially not if it was divided into 12 different bags. Especially not if those bags were labelled with the initials of their friends.

Lolz01: so we're good to go? You can do the plan tomorrow?

TayTay: if i go to school tomorrow yeah

What was this now?

Lolz01: r u not gonna go to school tomorrow? How come?

TayTay: its just so shit
TayTay: ive got history tomorrow and thats always the worst
TayTay: angela spends the whole class whispering to me that im fat and that no one wants to have sex with me and she gets her mate rob to join in and he tells me how ugly i am and benson just pretends he cant hear
TayTay: its true i am fat and ugly
TayTay: no one will ever want to touch me
TayTay: like I KNOW
TayTay: i see it in the mirror all the time
TayTay: they dont need to tell me
TayTay: but it hurts so much

Maureen had to shut her eyes. But when she did, all she could see was Laura. She opened her eyes again as the messenger app pinged.

TayTay: i rlly wish u went to my school

Without thinking, Maureen typed.

Lolz01: my dad said maybe i could transfer at sixth form
Lolz01: so perhaps next year

TayTay: OMG really???
TayTay: that would be so sick!!!

Taylor sent a string of smiling emoticons and warmth rushed through Maureen's body. Maybe this was what molly felt like? Maureen had to admit to being a tiny bit curious. Right now, however, making Taylor happy was the only illicit drug she needed.

Lolz01: so we've got a plan, right?
Lolz01: I promise u, they'll leave u alone forever once this is done

TayTay: yeah?

Lolz01: Yeah.

***

That awful day hadn't felt awful when Maureen had been on her way home. She had won three match points, picked up some of the Gu puddings Laura loved, turned up the Kinks on the car radio. The night before, Laura had come out of her room to watch TV, had even joined in House of Games, laughing and shouting out answers. Maureen hoped they were turning a corner.

The house had been so quiet that Maureen wondered if Laura had gone out with some friends. Her heart soared at the thought. "Laura!" she called, huffing up the stairs. "Are you there?" No reply.

So Maureen had opened her bedroom door, hoping to find it empty. But instead, she had seen the worst sight imaginable. The sight she would see every time she closed her eyes for the rest of her life.

While she had been out winning three games of tennis, her granddaughter had been writing a note, standing on a chair and tying a dressing gown cord around her neck. Just as Maureen had been throwing her arms in the air and shouting 'not bad for an old bird', Laura had kicked the chair away.

Maureen screamed, and dropped the shopping, the Gu puddings smashing on the floor. She ran to her granddaughter. She got the chair upright, clambered onto it, tried to lift Laura up. But even though she was so small, she was too heavy. Maureen tried to heave and heft her, but it couldn't be done, and anyway, it was clearly, so clearly, too late.

Even in the note, Laura didn't name the monsters who had done this to her. Even in death, she was still scared of them.

Well, Maureen wasn't scared of anything.

Not anymore.

***

WhatsApp was quiet.

She had played her part. Rung the school, left an anonymous complaint about Angela Edwards on the answering machine, to be picked up in the morning. Now, she was waiting. Maureen tidied her desk, dusting Laura and Peter's pictures. Laura was smiling, but Peter looked disapproving. Briefly, Maureen put him face down. But she couldn't leave him like that, so she stood the photo up again.

Maureen went through to the sitting room. It was nearly 5. Taylor was always home by now, always. Maybe WhatsApp had pinged, but she hadn't heard it? She shuffled back to the office – but no, the laptop was still blank.

Back to the sitting room. Could something have gone wrong? Could Taylor have been caught on her way to school? She said she had hidden all the bags of molly in the secret pocket of her bag, but someone could have found them. What if a teacher had seen her, or one of the other girls? What if she had decided that she wanted to try to drugs and they had killed her? What if she was being rushed to hospital, foaming at the mouth, eyes rolling back in her head? And then Maureen would be responsible for the death of two teenage girls. Unable to protect Laura while she was still alive, unable to defend her after she had died. What if Taylor had –

PING.

Oh thank goodness. Back into the office, as quickly as she could manage.

TayTay: hey!!!!!

Lolz01: hey!!! R u ok?

TayTay: yeah!!! i did it!

Lolz01: Yeah? And ur OK? Ur home?

TayTay: yeah. took me a while cos I had 2 wait till everyone went home
TayTay: waited in the library after classes
TayTay: then went and did it
TayTay: got into angelas locker no probs
TayTay: just shoved the package in
TayTay: shut the locker again and got out of there
TayTay: OMG she is gonna get in so much trouble!!!!!
TayTay: ur a genius i would never have thought of doing this!!!!!

Lolz01: and no-one saw u?

TayTay: nah no one was left in school
TayTay: i mean theres like a cctv camera in that corridor that benson is always threatening us with but everyone knows there isnt really any film in it

Cold fear clutched Maureen's throat. CCTV?

TayTay: u still there hon?

They had CCTV in schools now? That was just – Orwellian. That couldn't be legal. Could it?

TayTay: srsly laura ur the best

Well, Taylor must be right. There wouldn't really be film in that camera. It would be fine. It had to be.

TayTay: and ur definitely coming to my school next year right?
TayTay: so we can do shit like this all the time?

With numb fingers, Maureen typed.

Lolz01: yeah, definitely. Can't wait.

TayTay: Laura ur my best friend

Laura always helped other girls.
She would have helped Taylor too, Maureen knew it.

TayTay: ur the only person i can really trust

Yanjanani L. Banda

Yanjanani Leya Kalaya Banda is a writer from Malawi. She holds a BA in Study of Women and Gender/Comparative Literature from Smith College in Massachusetts, and finished courses for a Master's degree in Political Science and Diplomacy from South Korea's Pusan National University. When not writing, she spends her time dreaming up designs and sewing for her fashion business *Yaya's Reversible Designs*; cooking and cleaning; hanging out with her husband; and occasionally curling up on the couch for some Forged In Fire episodes or Track and Field events. Contrary to expectations, she is not athletic.

Welcome to Otherhood

You stifle a laugh when the girl with the caramel-colored skin tells you of the young men and women who run petrified at her melanin in the country of your dreams. It is not her you find funny. Or their running.

You wonder to yourself if the dark brown of your skin will solicit far much worse; so you muse at the power that the covering you have always walked in holds.

After all, you survived America. Where your first brush with its free people on the day of your arrival was praise for your fine, deep brown in a thick patois-laced American English as you walked the streets of Crown Heights.

You chuckled at the compliment. At the same time realizing that indeed you had arrived. In the place where your skin was the first thing people saw of you.

You remember terror-filled bus rides, sometimes, from the mall in the small town where you attended college; pictures with friends on night outs that made you realize the extent of your blackness; and anonymous letters slid under doors asking the monkeys to go back where they had come from.

You remember your "African American" professor's comments afterwards. To treat college like a grocery store.

"Pick out what you want and leave," he says, *"without minding the other stuff that might only distract you".*

You remember that white friend of a friend; and her apology when she fails to remember the other language spoken in Ethiopia where she had taught English for a couple of months.

You look at her with bewilderment in your eyes.

You wonder why she assumes that it is something you must know, and therefore, something she dare not forget.

You did not know there was another language spoken in Ethiopia apart from Amharic.

A part of you wants to commend her for knowing something you didn't. But you linger. Taking offense at her assumptions, and the guilt of your ignorance.

You ask yourself if you must carry the weight of the whole continent on your shoulders. If every nook and cranny of the motherland is yours to know and defend.

But you and your African friends also laugh sometimes. About terse responses of coming to America riding on a hippo and living with lions in your backyards.

The three day blackout due to the snow storm and the screams at night from your American friends make you feel invincible; and somewhat ashamed that you wear your continent's mediocrity like a superpower.

And before you perform the flower-salpuri, you lock yourself in the bathroom, scrubbing hard at your face in attempts to remove the ghostly white foundation covering your skin.

You are the only black girl on the team but your teacher wants you to blend in with everyone else; so you sit there wondering why you love the things that hate everything you are.

But that was America.

You leave for Korea of the South quite ready to excuse and forgive.

As you pack, you make sure you have enough foundation and powder for your dark skin. No one knows when you will have the opportunity to come back home, so you buy in bulk to avoid the inconvenience of humiliation.

You choose not to notice the stares, if ever they are any. But you finally have your date with the moment you had imagined.

When she sees you and your friends while already halfway across the bridge, she purposes to run back from whence she came. Her boyfriend switches sides and holds her tight as she shuts her eyes in an attempt not to scream as you pass each other by.

A part of you wants to inch even closer on the already small walkway to see just how much she will flinch. Her legs are like jelly, so you find yourself relenting.

"Do you think it's only your kind in the world?", you want to ask her.

But you reason with yourself. That this is indeed the extent of her world. And that real life beats the experience of their favorite Ghanaian turned Korean entertainer on TV. So you walk on. Wishing you could tell her to thank God for the restraint in you.

Others of her people take you to church. They feed you, show you around town, and offer you language lessons. But everything comes to a head when you don't want to go to their big Christmas gathering.

You lie to the lady that you have other plans so you cannot come. She tells you to cancel your plans. And even offers to make the call to your friend that will better explain why you are canceling those plans to begin with.

You find yourself inflamed with anger at the audacity in her to make you want to do what she wants.

Somewhere in her voice you can read the anger at what she assumes is your ungratefulness. At having eaten and drunk her cup of kindness and refusing to dance when she plays her flute of claim.

Yet you refuse to give in.

Your friends attempt to talk you into rethinking your decision; but you know that this battle of wills is yours for the taking. That this will be the last she ever sees of you after you had already stopped receiving of her hand.

When you walk out of the cafeteria that afternoon, it is with the finiteness of a world torn asunder. As you repeat to yourself that you will not be guilted into doing what you do not have the slightest interest in getting done.

That you will not wear the chains of the supposed poverty of everyone on your continent and the consequences of what your arms so readily received in their naïveté.

Instead, you roam in solitude. Longing for the future you left behind where everything had shattered, and only shards remained, as not for the faint of heart.

Bus and train rides to markets, restaurants, and other shopping destinations occupy your time. You relish the smiles, compliments, and *sobiseu* from *ahjummas* when they hear you speak in their tongue.

They can almost swear it is a native person speaking when you let out your perfectly rehearsed, yet limited Korean lines.

Only the fact that you can say anything at all in their mother tongue matters to their tender hearts. So they give you more tomatoes, meat, and vegetables in return.

You find yourself warming up to their not knowing. When they ask you where you are from, you are happy to tell them of your very little known country almost in the South, but also somewhere in the East, just below Tanzania.

Tanzania they are familiar with, you come to learn. So it becomes your reference point every time you have to speak of where you are from, which is often.

You enjoy the challenge of acting as an ambassador for your home.

But you also have to explain yourself when they hear you speak in English. They wonder if the people from your country also have an American accent like you do.

You do not like to explain yourself just as much as you do not like them assuming that you consciously decided to imitate the America of their dreams. A part of you feels short of the ambassadorial duties you place on yourself.

Your tongue is something you yourself cannot explain to yourself; even though you remember your French teacher asking you if you had ever lived in France the first time he heard you speak.

You learn to numb yourself to the questions and standards. The heavy, plain, and dark you is no match for the skinny, tall, and fair of the country of your dreams – and the world, really.

You wear your "not single" status as a shield from the sniding remarks of those of your gender. Those who, intentionally or otherwise open the wounds of everything you have tried to forget.

And when you sit across from your friend who takes his time to chew as he gushes over his now porcelain white skin that those from his country would appreciate, it occurs to you that it is your dark brown indirectly under attack. But you are calmer about it all.

You congratulate him on what feels like a great achievement as you tell him you cannot imagine yourself any other way.

Somehow he reminds you of your four years in America; and how you had fancied a much darker skin of a friend from Sudan amidst the chaos of the exhibition of blackness.

You cannot remember a moment where you wished you could crawl out of the blackness of your skin.

Soon you find yourself dealing with more than just skin. When you undo the braids on your teeny weeny afro, you find yourself in a crisis on what to do next.

The comfortable-with-short-hair woman in you walks around in hopes of finding someone to cut your hair. You find yourself going round and round as you pass every barbershop, certain that every one of them will not know what to do with you.

You contemplate taking a scissor to what now feels like your pain, but you brave your bias anyway and walk into the one with the lady inside.

She is kind. But when you come out, you regret the apologies for the hair that has always grown out of your scalp. Moments like these are a reminder of how the country of your dreams remains quite untouched by those of your kind.

When you finally make a Korean friend, you are grateful for her Kenyan experience. She tells you about the women of Kenya and making beads; of adventures in the bustling Nairobi and her desire to go back.

She has two kids now and wishes for an opportunity to have her family visit Kenya, and perhaps, your country too!

Her two sons do not stare at you like others do, and call you auntie without a second thought.

You call her *eonni* like you are supposed to. But for you, it is with a tenderness of so much more that you cannot explain.

It is your way of fighting off remarks like *"wakanda forever"* from possibly well-meaning professors.

On the subway, you pretend not to notice when they take videos of you. Yet other times you give them your back as your act of defiance.

Some of them touch your hair without ever even saying a word. You wonder to yourself if you seem more like a stray cat in need of a little bit of petting.

And just like in America, you find yourself in fear when the man who mumbles to himself leaves his seat and chooses to pace where you are standing on the train. You try to avoid eye contact and look out the door as you mutter under your breath for God to protect you.

Later when you tell your friend, you are aware of your shaking hands and resolve. But you tell her you would still choose Korea of the South over America. That America's hostility to the likes of you and her spans centuries of living in the same country while that is not the case where you are.

But it does not wash away the disdain that overtakes you when the woman at the gym in the mountains pretends to shake your hand in greeting just to examine the dark brown of your hands. She flips and pulls at your hands and fingers, and caresses your face with an entitlement that makes your skin crawl.

You want to scream your lungs out at her audacity. At her indifference to a scrutiny that would equally send her over the edge. But you find yourself back to muttering *"God help me"* under your breath.

You ask yourself why God chooses to speak to your heart; telling you to calm down instead of telling the likes of her not to examine you like a doll on a shop display.

With the battle raging within you, you flash your rehearsed smile that signals something like understanding.

You gently pull your hand away and move as far as you can go; away from the prying eyes of *ahjummas* and *ahjussis* who had been your comfort zone once upon a time. All the while asking yourself if you had done a disservice to others of your kind. Those who would stand where you stood as your hand endured an ounce of the attraction of Sarah Baartman's freak show.

And when your eight-year-old English student asks you why your palm is dark, you find yourself firing back with why her own is white. But you know that your anger is not for her.

You can excuse her not knowing, although to what extent you do not know.

Later, when you try to get a tutoring job for a three-year-old, you find yourself embarrassed when she cries. Scared, perhaps, that your darkness might consume her.

Crouched on the floor of her parents apartment, it occurs to you that you will have to say the words. To ease the embarrassment splattered across her mother's face as she tries to get her daughter to see that you are just like her, only darker. And perhaps, nothing to be feared.

You stop the tears from coming out of your eyes. It is not regret at wearing your skin.

With the bravest voice you can muster, you release her mother from the shame of the moment. And walk out with your thoughts in shambles as to how you will survive.

You wish there was a clear line drawn in the sand. One that marked out ignorance from the sheer brutality of the gazes where you are the object. So that you could also ask why they came out unbaked even though you came out burnt.

And when you find yourself an unwilling spokesperson of the

enslaved of your continent in your World History class; one to perform the pain and welcome the pity for the recounted atrocities of "fruits" thrown overboard for an insurance claim while saving white lives; you gather your books and bag with a finality characteristic of your mother's blood.

You take a bow, books clutched in hand, and start for a home where *other* is just a different kind.

Leah Carter

Leah Carter is a middle-grade and short story writer from Tauranga, New Zealand. Her junior manuscript was shortlisted for the Storylines New Zealand Tom Fitzgibbon Award in 2021. She aspires to seeing her name on the middle-grade shelf in bookstores. Her short stories have been shortlisted (Tasmanian Writers' Prize, Secret Lives Short Story Competition, An Axe to Grind flash fiction) and longlisted (Flash 500). Leah lives a hybrid existence juggling her day job, teenage dramas, and writing in every spare minute.

Cat Got Your Tongue

Only one person knows what happened that day.

It's a small town. I knew him, of course. Everybody did. Eli worked at the run-down petrol station on the corner of Mill Road and the highway. He was popular with the locals; people had nothing but kind words to say about him. Friendly smile, helpful, an honest-to-God good guy.

Mrs Rogers from the second-hand shop reckoned Eli could sense her coming. Said he was half-way out the door when she drove onto the forecourt in her Mini coupe, fluffy-dice dangling from the rear-vision mirror. He'd have the petrol pump in his hand before she got the chance to pull up the handbrake. Charmed her with his boyish grin. Had an impeccable employment record. Never had any dramas.

Except that one time when Roy Goodman went in to complain about the petrol price. Roy was always going on about it. Bloody oil companies ripping everyone off. He thought it was criminal. The story goes that Roy marched up to the counter, made finger guns and began shooting. Pow-pow-pow. People said he was wearing a cowboy hat. Must have looked a right sight, an 83-year-old cowboy shooting up a petrol station with his fingers. I think he was trying to say those oil company bastards should be shot, but who knows. He was hard to follow, that Roy Goodman. May he rest in peace.

Anyway, it must have spooked Eli because he completely lost his cool, so they say. Went off at Roy, called him a stupid motherfucker, and told him to get the hell out of there. Scared the living shit out of poor old Roy. For the last year of his life, he had to drive almost fifty kilometres to get his petrol.

People were wary of Eli after that. For a while, anyway. Conversation was limited to the weather and what people were up to in the weekend. There were no more signs of anything fiery lurking under the surface, so the Roy Goodman incident was forgotten.

***

I remember the day Hannah Davis arrived in town. She had a mass of dark crinkled hair and skin darker than mine. She strolled into the café in her townie clothes and asked for a decaf soy latte with cream. *Cream? With a soy latte?* She shot me a dark look, so I made her the drink.

She sat alone by the window. Usually the young ones that come into the café are attached to their phones, tapping and swiping, but not Hannah. Her head swivelled back and forth like she was watching a tennis game. Every time a car stopped outside, she'd eye the door like she was expecting Michelle Obama to step out. She'd quickly look the other way when it turned out to be Mrs Rogers or one of the other townsfolk.

I was replenishing the scones in the front cabinet when Eli ambled across the highway toward the café. Hannah spotted him too. Her eyes lingered, taking in his tall lanky frame and faded jeans hanging so low I could see his boxers.

Eli didn't so much as glance in her direction. He waltzed up to the counter with a cheery smile. I didn't give him the chance to speak.

"The usual?"

He nodded. "Thanks Beth."

I grabbed a brown paper bag and slipped a sausage roll with a sachet of tomato sauce inside.

"Mmm, those scones smell good. Maybe I'll get one of those next time."

I smiled. "How's your day going?"

"Bit slow. Nothing much to report."

Eli had been working at that petrol station since he left school. I never figured out why he stayed. Everyone knew his struggles, growing up. He was little when his mother left. We all felt for Eli, being brought up by his dad. He wasn't exactly father-of-the-year material, what with his drinking problem and all.

Eli pulled his wallet out, ready to pay, when I heard sobbing sounds coming from the table by the window. Eli spun around. Hannah was slumped over, full-on crying like her childhood pet had died. Her crazy-big hair was spread out over the table, bobbing up and down as she wept.

Eli turned to face me. "Who's that?"

I shrugged.

He hurried over to her, leaving his sausage roll on the counter. He pulled up a chair and sat down. I wasn't surprised. He was like that. I remember when Mrs Rogers tripped over the welcome mat at the petrol station. Max, the owner, said Eli had propped her up, wrapped an ice-pack around her ankle and made her a cup of tea.

I don't know what Eli said to Hannah that day, but whatever it was, it worked. Before long, the two of them were smiling and laughing like old friends. From that day on, they were inseparable. Over the following months, she hung around the café every morning, waiting for him to show up for his tea break.

Didn't take long for word to get out Hannah was staying at the Henderson place about a kilometre down the road. Had been empty for years, since old Mr Henderson died. Pete, our local constable, paid her a visit. Turned out Mr Henderson had left the house to Hannah's mum in his will. Hannah could have said anything though; it wasn't like anyone was going to check. Constable Pete and the rest of us townsfolk went about our business, not too worried if her story was true or not. Besides, that old house had been an eyesore for years. Hannah spruced up the place – she painted the fence, weeded the garden, cleaned up the rubbish. She breathed life into it.

Given it's a small town, it didn't take long for word to get out about Eli staying over. I'd spot him strolling along the highway early in the morning on his way to work. Thing was, his place was about three kilometres in the other direction, so it didn't take a genius to work out what was going on. His dishevelled appearance – shirt half tucked in, just-got-out-of-bed hair, wearing the same clothes as the day before. Big smile on his face though.

In the café, we ribbed him about being a ladies' man, but he'd ignore us. He'd order a sausage roll, eyes fixed on Hannah beaming at him from the table by the window. He'd scurry off and we'd whisper amongst ourselves behind the counter. Ah, to be young again. That intoxicating honeymoon phase.

She reminded me of a movie-star with her exotic look and flashy clothes. Eli looked like a small-town kid with buck teeth from Hicksville. Never quite knew what she saw in him. Guess we'll never know.

***

Everyone in town has a story from that day. We all remember different things, have a different take on what happened.

I was driving to the café that morning, when I saw him wandering along the road ahead. I assumed he was on his way to work. There's no footpath along that part of the highway; I slowed to a crawl so I didn't scare him. He had a curious sway to his walk, but I figured he was tripping over his jeans since they were hanging off him. As I cruised past, I lifted my hand off the steering wheel to wave.

Eli didn't react. He stared blankly ahead, zombie-like. I peered into the rear-vision mirror for another look and that's when I noticed something on his T-shirt. At first, I thought he'd been splashed with mud by a passer-by. I pulled over, thinking he may need a lift. I waited for him to catch up.

He approached the car and for a moment I thought he was going to walk on by. Then he stopped abruptly next to the passenger door and leaned into the open window.

"Beth," he said.

He spoke calmly, like nothing was out of the ordinary. My heart sped up as I studied him.

His T-shirt, once white, was soaked red across the front. There was a large, concentrated patch of crimson, surrounded by lighter-coloured smears. Specks of red were on his arms, his hands, his face. A faint metallic smell hung in the air between us.

The engine was running. Part of me wanted to slam my foot on the accelerator and hightail it out of there. Instead, I sat there, frozen.

"Beth," he said, again.

He smiled, an eerie smile. My eyes stayed transfixed on his.

A car whizzed past and I flinched.

"Cat got your tongue?" he said.

Something flickered in his eyes. Was he... amused? I pushed the thought aside. Course not. Must have been my imagination.

"Jesus, Eli. What happened?"

His demeanour changed; the glimmer in his eyes vanished. He looked like a boy caught stealing money from his dad's wallet.

"What?" he said, gingerly.

"The blood, Eli. What's going on?"

He held out his hands and gasped, like he was seeing the blood for the first time. He let out a long guttural groan and sank to the ground, out of sight.

I turned the engine off, leapt out of the car and hurried to him. He knelt by the passenger door, rocking back and forth, his face tucked into his knees like he was praying.

I squatted down next to him and lightly patted his shoulder. My brain was shrouded in a thick fog. My scrambled thoughts darted all over the place.

We stayed like that for a few minutes. As he wailed, his body bucked and jerked like there was something deep inside him, clambering to get out.

Finally, I said, "Wait there, Eli. I need to get help."

It was like someone slapped him in the face. He sprung up, all cat-like, and brushed the dirt off his jeans. "I've got to get to work," he mumbled, and took off down the road.

He was staggering, mind you, like he was drunk.

"Eli!" I yelled, but he didn't look back. I got into my car and rang Constable Pete. I was stammering, barely able to get out a coherent sentence.

"Stay there," said Pete, evenly. "Keep an eye on him, but don't approach. I'm on my way."

I watched Eli stumble along the highway toward town. It was only when I saw the flashing police lights in the distance that I noticed my trembling hands on the steering wheel.

***

Gossip was rife around town about what happened.

"I was talking to Eleanor," said Mrs Rogers, eyeing the scones on the café's counter. She checked over her shoulder, then leaned in. "Her kitchen overlooks the Henderson's driveway, and she saw a car pull in about six o'clock. Said a big burly bloke got out and banged on the front door, real angry like."

"To have here?" I asked, pointing at the scones.

Mrs Rogers nodded. "Constable Pete said he was Hannah's boyfriend. Tracked her down, apparently."

I plated up the scone, butter on the side and no relish, the way she liked it.

"He was a real piece of work, according to Pete," she said. "Been in trouble with the law. Gang connections and all that."

I pushed the plate toward her and punched the buttons on the till.

"They reckon he pulled a knife on Eli and Hannah. Eli was lucky to get out alive. Pete reckons it was a case of wrong place, wrong time for poor Eli. He's a good kid. Always been a great help to me at the petrol station. I'll never forget the day he helped me when I tripped over the welcome mat."

She spun around when the café door jangled behind her. One-legged Sam Thompson, who worked at the bookshop, shuffled up to the counter. She leaned in closer.

"Pete said the crime scene was a real mess. Blood everywhere," she whispered. "He must have been in a terrible state of shock when you bumped into him on the highway. Anyways, you have a good day now." She picked up her scone, and turned to Sam. "Morning," she said cheerily, then headed to a far-corner table. I stared after her.

"Excuse me, Beth?"

Sam studied me curiously from the other side of the counter.

"Sorry, Sam. I was miles away. Right, what can I get for you?"

***

I was crouched down, topping up the tray of caramel slice, when I saw Eli walk across the road toward the café. I watched his cheery grin get closer, through the thick cabinet glass.

I knew it was a matter of time before he would be back at the petrol station. He'd been released on bail. Everyone around town was convinced it was self-defence; that he'd used justified force to defend himself. Most people predicted a full acquittal of the manslaughter charge.

He yanked open the door and strolled up to the counter. I took a long, deep breath and stood up, ready to greet him.

"Beth," he said.

I was immediately transported back to that moment on the road when he'd spoken my name in the same soft tone. I could picture his face peering at me through the car window. I recalled the chill that came over me when he'd held my stare. *Cat got your tongue?* A strange choice of words when splattered in someone else's blood.

I studied him from across the counter. Who was he? The honest-to-God good guy Mrs Rogers believed him to be, or was he hiding a darker side? What of the story when he'd lost his shit with old Roy

Goodman and his finger guns those years back?

"Beth," he repeated. His sunny smile was gone, his eyes dark and intense. My breathing quickened. My mouth was dry. My heart hurried. I curled my fingers into fists to stop the trembling.

"The usual?" I asked calmly.

He nodded.

I picked up the sausage roll with the tongs and slipped it into the brown paper bag with a sachet of sauce.

"Thanks Beth," he grinned.

Rosie Garland

Rosie Garland has a passion for language nurtured by public libraries. She writes long and short fiction, poetry and sings with post-punk band The March Violets. Her latest poetry collection *What Girls do in the Dark* (Nine Arches Press) was shortlisted for the Polari Prize 2021. Her novel *The Night Brother* (Borough Press) was described by *The Times* as "a delight... with shades of Angela Carter." Val McDermid has named her one of the most compelling LGBT+ writers in the UK today. http://www.rosiegarland.com/

Happy Ever After With Bear

The road trip is going long. We steer clear of the phrase *running away* in case it breaks the spell. I know about spells. My father read a bedtime story where the prince was a bear until someone said *hey, you're a bear* and crack, the magic broke apart and he was back in his ordinary body and it was supposed to be a perfect ending.

You shift gear and machinery grinds. If not for you and this car I'd be stuck in a hungry life that had chewed me to the bone. I knew we had a chance when I said, *I don't sleep nights* and you said *OK*. Not *Why?* or *That's stupid*, or *You can do anything if you want to badly enough.*

The car stinks, an animal odour that blooms in the evening, and though we've never managed to pin down where it's coming from, I'm guessing it's me. I love the rankness; everything a journey should be, away from that and towards this.

I drag a blanket from the back, choked with dog hair. My father said we had hairy hearts, me and him, which was what made us warm. I wondered what my mother's was made of. She won the custody case, not because she loved me, but because she hated him.

Grr, I say.

Woof, you reply, gunning the engine.

The headlights sweep a stand of trees and I see faces looming out of the bark and because we promised no secrets, I tell you. You peer into the shadows and say, *it's ok, they're good trees. Friendly faces.*

We crest the hill and break free from the tree line. My heart is quaking like a newborn lamb. I'm in awe of the way they stagger upright within minutes of being born, racing around a moment after. In that fairy tale where the prince was a bear, he had a stag inside him. Inside the stag was a wolf, and inside the wolf was a fox, and inside the fox was a lamb, heart skittering. I've never minded the leaping inside my chest.

Sun's coming up. You ruffle the hair cropped over my ears, the stubble trying my chin for size. You believe in me, whatever shape I'm in. Never once have you said, *hey, you're a bear* and broken the spell. Never once asked *Are you feeling more human?* as though that's all there is to aim for.

It's time for me to take the wheel. To look out of the window and think about how love is holding back on questions we can't answer. Love is the drive, the car, the road, unrolling.

Paddy Gillies

Paddy Gillies lives on a farm in a remote reach of Devon. His short fiction has been recognised by the Bridport Prize, the Bath Flash Fiction Award, Reflex Fiction, Cranked Anvil, Flash500 and Retreat West. He is currently working on a novel and a stage play. He is undertaking a master's degree at Cambridge University.

Ghosts of the Wind River Valley

They sat side by side, a little way apart, on the only chairs in the room. High, beech, ladder-backed chairs that were about the only thing he had inherited from his father. They watched the news in silence. The girl had gone missing sometime the day before. Never made it to school. Her folks had known something was wrong by the time the afternoon bell rang. Everyone else knew by nightfall.

'Why do these things happen?' She asked.

When he woke she rested her hand on his chest as if she could keep him there. Downstairs she heard him turn on the radio in the kitchen. The weather forecast. She waited to see which way it would go, knowing already.

In the yard he led the older horse into the trailer and hitched it to the post ring, giving it room to throw its head if it needed. He bent to lift the ramp, the spot on his hip flaring as he rose and pushed the door fast. The dark was leaching out of the sky and to the east the horizon bruised purple. The wind had turned a few hours before. A roof sheet had come loose on the hay barn and slapped hard against the rafters. They said the first twenty-four hours were the most important. He didn't know much about that but he did know that if the child was outside when the north-easterly brought those first goose-grey, pregnant clouds then it wouldn't go well.

Marcie came through the gate, her hat pulled down around her ears and held out a flask. He shook his head.

'I'll take some now.'

He unscrewed the cap and poured a half cup into it. The bitter scald traced a route inside him. He saw her look past him at the rifle leaning against the truck.

'I guess I'll see you when I see you.'

She nodded and stepped forward, reached up with a gloved hand and kissed him on the cheek. She made to speak but he had turned away.

'Good luck.'

He looked back at her for a moment and nodded. She inclined her head slightly; over the barns, beyond the low meadows and up towards the hills. Into the wind and what it was bringing.

'Be careful.'

At the bridge he picked his way through the cruisers, an ambulance and the many trucks like his. He parked up and walked back to the group standing by the sheriff's car. They had a map spread on the bonnet and talked in low, morning voices.

'Kaspar.'

He nodded back at the sheriff, and some of the others said his name and nodded at him.

'They got a chopper coming out of Riverton but we don't know how much we can get out of it before the weather comes in. The best we can do is cover some of the lower ground while we can. Anyplace you want to try?'

He pointed down at the map. The sheriff tilted his head to one side like he was listening to a child trying to get something right but just missing.

'Whatever you think. You know the country as good as anyone. Most of us going to concentrate along the river road. You want to come with us?'

The shapes of the trees were starting to slip from the darkness as he walked back to the truck.

'Kaspar. You armed?'

He raised his hand as he went.

He saddled the horse in the trailer. Her ears were pricked but she was steady. It's why he'd brought her and not one of the colts. It was a day for not making mistakes. He backed her down the ramp talking quietly as they went. Vehicles were starting up. Far below he could see the lights from the ore smelter and the town beyond.

The television said she came from one of the streets down by the glass factory. Streets where most of the headlines came from. The mother had rocked slightly next to the police chief, her face hollowed as she'd made her appeal. They'd found some messages on her computer. They didn't think she was alone.

Ahead was wild country. No road for sixty or seventy miles he reckoned. The way had been built by the men who had come searching for silver, years before even his grandfather had been born. No trace of them now except some stone chimneys and the path. The naked alder and buckeye branches twitched in the wind and back among the rocks he saw a wild apple tree stencilled against the pale stones. He thought of the pear in the field by the stream, below the house. A sheltered spot that trapped the sun in summer. When they were younger they used to lie in the long grass there, listening to the water. His head on her lap. Then, when things went wrong the third time, and there had been enough to bury, he had dug a small depression in the thin, root-riddled soil. They had placed the spotless, white, swaddled parcel in the dirt and covered it with stone and dust. There was no marker. Just the two of them knew. In the early years he had seen her sitting there sometimes, on her own. Sideways on, her legs tucked under her. Her fingers tracing on the ground like she was drawing or writing. He hadn't seen that for a very long time. He had not walked through that field for an age. Just put the ewes who came on late, in there at the end of the season. It was a safe place for them while they weaned. He would lean on the gate and count them and the lambs. Never seemed to lose any down there. They grew well in those last days of summer as the swallows pitched over the river bank and the blossom on the old tree had set into small, hard pods that began to form up. They had never spoken about not trying again. It had just seemed to happen after a few years. Like they both knew there was nothing more to be done. She didn't stop coming to him in the night, pushing across the bed and reaching for his face in the darkness. It was just that the whole thing seemed to mean something else by then.

At the top of the first rise he could see for two, maybe three miles. There was no tree cover. Just rocks and bluegrass, dogbane and small, shuddering bushes of sagebrush. Higher, snow from the last storm. He wondered how far a girl that age could walk. How badly she wanted to get away from town, from home. Or how far someone was willing to take her. What they wanted from a place.

As they neared the beginning of the high ridge he got down and held the horse. A piece of foil fluttered and settled. He picked it up and turned it in his fingers. A candy wrapper. Old paper didn't just blow around for ever. It settled, got caught up, turned dull and brittle. He pulled out his phone but there had been no signal for a few miles now. He wondered what sort of man would take someone like that. When they had lost their balance, when they had tilted and their centre of gravity had spun out. Or maybe they had never had it. Something touched his eyelid and then his lip. The tiniest of flakes skittered in the air. He looked forward, guessing the distances and times. The sky was the grey of river pebbles, further north, darker. He looked at the wrapper and then tucked it into his pocket. He remounted, looked back over his shoulder and then nudged the mare with his heels.

Ahead the ground pinched up into four stony peaks. There were rounded pits in some of the rocks up there. The kitchens of ancient people. Then beyond, the fold in the valley where the last stones of the miners' camp lay scattered. Worm-eaten fragments of their cabins fossilising like bleached bones.

The snow came on hard when he was halfway across the talus. The horse had to search for footing as the ground disappeared. At the foot of the final rise he swung from the stirrups and slid down her wet flank, landing heavily. Heat seared his hip. He pressed his gloved finger against the small round welt of scar tissue. They found some shelter on the lea side and he tied her to a stub of aspen growing in the rock face. He rested his hand on her muzzle and said a few words then turned into the wind and snow.

At the summit he took off the rifle and unclipped the plastic cap from the scope. He moved the crosshair slowly across the ledge below. Something dark moved. He couldn't see clearly in the swirl. He sealed the sight and walked on slowly.

The man was hanging from a rusted old spike that had been driven into the rock a hundred years ago or more. The belt had cinched tight into the flesh and the fingers of his right hand were trapped under the edge of the leather where it cut into the folds of his skin. Like he'd changed his mind. He was young. He turned slowly in the wind, revolving one way then the other. There was no bird damage to him. He scanned for track but knew that the storm would have covered anything well before. At the end of the rock wall were the remains of a building. She was sitting on a small cairn of stones watching him approach. Something caught in his throat and for a moment he felt unsteady, as if his feet were going to give. The thinness of the air left him lightheaded. He understood that he had never believed that this moment was going to happen. Had always kept the alternative outcome close. As if expecting it might ward off its occurrence. He took a step forward and stopped.

'You ok?'

She nodded.

'You hurt?'

She shook her head. She was wearing a light jacket. The sort of coat you'd pick out on a spring morning. Her face was pink raw. He walked up to her. She didn't move. He didn't know what to do.

'I'm Kaspar.'

He reached out his hand and she hesitated, then shook it. The snow was falling thicker again.

'You hungry?'

She nodded.

'I got food. It's back with my horse. We'll go get it.'

She stood and together they walked back along the bluff. When they got to the hanging man he watched her as she took a glance up and then continued at his side. A little way on he stopped. He walked back to the man, took out his knife and sawed through the belt. The body keeled away and for one moment stood upright before it fell sideways into the snow. He rolled it onto its back and tried to close the eyelids but they were frozen stiff. He stood looking at the dead man for a moment then walked back to the girl. She was watching, her dark eyes expressionless.

The snow fell again in dense swathes and he knew it had been a mistake to leave the food with the horse. He took off his hat and handed it to the girl. He needed to get her out of the weather. About halfway across he fell. He lay for a moment, his cheek against the cold and the wet of the snow. The girl stood above him.

'You ok?'

It was the first time she had spoken. He nodded back at her.

'Just old and stupid. But there ain't no cure for that.'

He thought he saw a glimmer of something on her face. The snow kept coming. In places his feet disappeared into drifts. Twice he had to lift her where it was too deep. She didn't flinch at his touch.

The horse called out when they reached it. It's rump, pushed into the weather, was crusted with ice. The girl reached up and stroked its head as he took down the bag from the saddle. He found a spot just beyond and cleared a space. When they had finished eating he stood and took the saddle off the horse. Underneath was a wool numnah. He sat down and pulled it over them.

'Are we staying here?'

'Yes. We can't go down. We'll get got by the cold or fall.'

'How long for?'

Her breath clouded in front of her face.

''Til the snow stops and they come looking for us.

'Who?'

'Half the town I'd say.'

She looked away from him and sat in silence.

'Did you come looking for me?'

'Yes. Yes I did.'

'Why?'

'To make sure you were safe.'

She said nothing. He looked into the blizzard. The light was fading now.

'Did he... did that man hurt you?'

She shook her head.

'Did he do anything...'

The words trailed off. She shook her head and he wondered how old a girl had to be to understand what was meant by that question. Not old enough he figured. Not too old at all. They sat in silence as the world turned white and grey. He looked at her face. Her eyes were watering and there was a tremor to her head.

'We need to keep you warm. You understand?'

She nodded and he reached around her pulling her close to him. He took off her wet gloves and gave her his. He joined his arms around her. They sat in silence for a while. He wanted her to stay awake.

'The people who lived here before folk like us arrived were called the Shoshone. The Grass House People some called them. On account they mostly lived on the plains.'

He sat lower and straightened his leg.

'One time I was fishing with some fellas out past Torrey Creek. I couldn't get on them trout so I went further, on my own. I found a place where the fish were keener. When it was getting to the end of the day and I needed to get back to the camp I got out of the water and saw something on the rock. I guess you could only see it when the light was a certain way. Like in the morning or just then, when the sun hit the stones in a particular way.'

Her eyes were open and she listened, her breath shallow.

'There was a woman scratched on that rock. She was staring right at me. She was holding things in her hands, round with little legs on them. I never seen anything like it.'

He didn't tell her that as he had stood there, in the valedictory burnish of the day, he had seen clearly the tears carved into the woman's face, trailing down from the orbs of her eyes. Her pain as she held him in her thousand year old gaze.

'Who was she?'

'I went to the library at Buffalo. First time since I was about your age I reckon. They found me a book. She was called Pa Waip. The book called her Water Ghost Woman. Said she could fire invisible arrows. Said she was a trickster and a healer. That she could lure men into the water but save them too. Some fella went into the river nearby a few years back. The book said he felt a hand pull him out and on to the bank. When he looked around there was no one there. He swears Pa Waip saved him.'

'What were the round things?'

'Turtles. She could tell the turtles what to do for her. She couldn't go on the land herself see?'

He didn't tell her that the book said some scholars thought they were the headless bodies of children she had drowned in the dark, night water.

'So was she good or bad?'

He could feel the faint warmth of her body.

'I guess she was both.'

'How can you be both?'

He thought of the rigid figure on the escarpment above them, its flawless white blanket. The hungers it had faced.

'I guess we all are.'

'Why?'

'Well I guess life is. Good and bad.'

He woke shivering hard. The night was black around them, the snow was falling harder than before. There was ice on his neck and the girl was shaking, half across his legs. For the first time he believed they were going to die.

He thought about the decisions he had made. The food he had not brought. The flares. The matches. He thought back to the times in the desert when the choice of track meant life or not. The decision to tie the tourniquets or to inject adrenalin, to put down cover fire or to bury your face in the sand and pray they couldn't see you. The choice of words in the letters he had sent. All of the settlements he had ever made. To walk up to her at the corn festival and ask her to dance. To bend down and offer the slim silver ring. To consign her to a life without that which she wanted most. Everything he had got wrong. He imagined them finding their bodies in the spring. The pyre of mistakes he has made threatened to engulf him. When he lost consciousness again he was chased by painted men on small palomino horses. He kept running and they kept getting closer until he reached the edge of the land and there was nowhere else to go.

When he opened his eyes it had stopped snowing. A few wisps traced helical patterns in front of him. Above he could see stars beyond the fraying clouds. The girl stirred and he pulled his hand from his sleeve and felt her face. It was marble cold. She looked about her. He pulled the last of the food from his pocket and passed it to her. She ate slowly.

She looked at him and then offered him the chocolate. He shook his head.

'You carry on. Old 'uns like me don't get hungry. Don't sleep, don't eat. Don't do much of anything.'

She finished in silence. He sat forward and winced as pain shot through his hip flexor, through his femur and into the core of him. She looked up.

'You hurt your leg?'

He nodded.

'Did you do it coming up here?'

'No. I did it a long time ago.'

'Why does it still hurt?'

'I guess it broke some things that can't be mended. I guess it will always hurt.'

'What did you do?'

'I didn't do nothing. Someone did it to me.'

'Who?'

'Just some people who thought they were on the side of right, just like I did.'

To the east, the faintest loosening of the night came at the edge of the hills. The sky was brilliant in the suffocating cold.

'What's the horse called?'

He told her and watched the mare standing stock still, head down.

'I've got some more if you ever want to come and see them. With your folks.'

She nodded.

Dawn threw a pale pink cast over the pristine ground. He looked at the sky. The clear window above and the dark to the north. He didn't want to make the decision. He glanced down at the girl and she looked back up at him, her face flushed. They had maybe an hour. He knew he had no choice.

He went first leading the mare, testing the drifts with a stick. When he couldn't feel the ground they changed direction. He kept the high peaks on their left and marked their elevation by the blue and anthracite strata on the cliff face.

On a slope of steep scree his feet went from under him. He let go of the reins and slid down. His hand caught on a stone and he stopped himself. His feet weren't touching the ground. He looked behind him and could only see white land a long way below.

The girl moved towards him.

'Don't come closer, you hear?'

He moved his feet trying to feel for purchase. He wondered if he went down here if they would find her before the next storm hit. If the horse would make it easier for them to spot her. He thought of Marcie. He remembered his father teaching him how to kill the steers. The brown eyes regarding him stolidly as he pressed the bolt gun onto their forehead. His father's impatience. And the young boy in the desert who had clung to his friend's torso as the blood soaked into him and the tracer latticed over their heads. How he had slapped him. Pulled him away by his flak vest and thrown him behind the sand bags. Told him there would be time for that later. But there never had been. He felt all his strength failing. He was breathing hard and the stone was cutting through his gloves into the tendons of his fingers. Something in him creased and he felt his chest empty. He felt the pull of gravity and the depth of the fall. How when he let go, that the fall might last forever. How his whole life had felt like this and for so long he had just held on. That he couldn't last any longer.

Then he felt the hand on his wrist. She was bending forward, one hand on him the other holding the reins. She was trying to pull him up. He reached out. She lay down and passed the rein around his right arm and knotted them like a child would.

'Stay away. I mean it.'

He chittered at the horse and it stepped backwards. The horse moved again and he felt himself slide slightly. His toes caught something. Then his knees were on stones. He lay in the snow and tears came. The girl stood a little way on next to the horse and watched. He lay there feeling the ground beneath him. He felt that he would meld into it. When he rolled onto his back he saw a White-tailed kite, high above, drifting in ever increasing circles.

A little after seven, when they had been walking for some time, he heard the helicopter. At first he thought it would pass too far to the west of them but it tilted and banked. It kept away, high enough not to disturb the snow, but he knew they'd been seen.

He recognised the first one. A young fella out of Worland. The other two he didn't know. They shrouded the two of them in foil and checked their fingers. They took the girl's boots off and examined her toes. None of them could stop grinning. One squeezed his arm so hard it hurt. At the end of the track others waited. The men were bursting with the good of life. They took the girl and put her on one of the quads. She looked back over her shoulder as it took her down and away.

Marcie knelt next to him, one hand resting on his thigh.

'You should have gone with them.'

'I'm ok.'

The fire let out a crack like a shot.

'Don't get too close.'

He nodded. He couldn't feel the heat yet. That pain was to come.

'You saved her. That little girl. She'd be dead without you.'

He lay his head back on the chair top and watched the flames. Outside he imagined the smoke curling up and over the farm. He rose with it. Above the barns and the meadow, over the stream and the small corner with the pear. Seeing everything he had ever gained and all he had ever lost.

Lizzie Golds

Lizzie Golds grew up in Ascot, England and now lives in Bristol. Her short stories have previously been published by *Dear Damsels, en bloc magazine* and mishmashfood.co.uk. She is currently studying part-time for an MA in Creative Writing alongside her day job as a copywriter. You can find her on Instagram and Twitter @lizzie_golds.

Sunshine Beach

You've lost her already. She is running away from you barefoot, propelling herself across the beach, kicking up the sand behind her without looking back.

'Cherry!' Your throat hurts. You don't have the lungs for shouting like she does. The wind whips your words away as soon as they leave your dry mouth. You follow behind her, staggering through the stitch in your right shoulder. 'We need to go. It's not safe.'

Even the hardcore surfers are packing up and leaving. They grew up knowing that the natural world could easily kill them. It is only just midday, but the sky is a darkening swirl of orange, purple and grey.

Cherry stops and turns around. She throws her arms out wide, tipping her head back and letting the wind rip at her clothes. She's not dressed for this weather. Neither are you. You're both wearing thin tops, shorts, flimsy summer things that rub and ride up and reveal strips of bare skin. The difference between you is that Cherry doesn't mind being unprepared. Actually, she loves the thrill of it. This is why you fell in love with her, this is why you'll lose her.

'It's fine!' she yells. 'I grew up in Devon.'

You catch up with her, your chest heaving. 'This is *not* Devon!'

Weather hits different in Australia. The rain here is nothing like the pissing excuse for rain at home. Back in Sydney, you and Cherry stood outside a bar during a downpour and caught golf-sized raindrops in pint glasses. You were both soaked through in less than five seconds. The bar staff thought you were mad, you thought it was hilarious. You went running through the city like a pair of sugared-up children, wet hands clasped together, hooting and screaming with laughter. Back at the hostel, Cherry held your face in her hands, steadied herself, and said, 'I think we're going to be alright.' Her breath smelled of vodka, you couldn't remember how many she'd had. Her pupils were so dilated that her eyes were almost black.

'We're going to be alright,' you repeated. But by that point, she was out of it. Her body crumpled into yours and you held her close, as close as you could.

You flew into Brisbane during a thunderstorm. The plane had to attempt its landing three times. Cherry dug her nails so hard into your skin when she gripped your hand that the red marks were still there a day later. The pain made your eyes water. You didn't tell her she hurt you. You didn't tell her you were scared too. You thought, then, that if you'd died right there, you'd have died happy. You would have already got everything you wanted from life. You would have already lived hard enough for a hundred lifetimes. You would have died knowing what it was to love someone with everything you had.

'You think I don't know that?' Cherry says now. The burnt sunlight is making her icy blonde hair look a blazing shade of copper. She almost dyed it that colour once – you think it would have suited her. 'That's why I love it here, it's nothing like home,' she says.

You've tried to ignore it, tried to skirt around it, tried to sweep it under every metaphorical carpet you could find – but you know Cherry doesn't want to leave. She's been talking about it for weeks. It started ten days into your trip, while you were sipping smoothies on

Tamarama Beach, cold metal straws clinking against your teeth.

'Maybe we could stay longer,' Cherry said, making waves in the air with her hand. 'Travel around a bit more.'

'We've still got time,' you said, swirling your straw around in your drink.

'Six weeks isn't that long.'

'I've already taken as much unpaid leave as I can.'

Cherry turned to you and pushed her sunglasses up onto her head. Her grey eyes had that faraway look about them again, like she was talking to you from somewhere else entirely, somewhere that would always be just out of your reach. 'Why don't we quit, then?'

You smiled at first, tried to humour her. Then you shook your head. The thing is: you love your job. You're part of a dying breed: a full-time journalist with an annual salary and a pension and a holiday allowance. You have a window desk with a succulent on it. You worked your arse off for it. It took years of unpaid internships, dogsbody coffee runs, second jobs in nightclubs filled with sleazy hands that wouldn't stop grabbing, solo walks home in the rain at night with your keys between your fingers. You gave your everything for that desk. 'I don't know, Cherry,' you said. 'I don't think so.'

Cherry got up and walked to the water's edge. You called after her, but she didn't turn around. She wouldn't talk to you for the rest of the afternoon.

Two weeks later, Cherry came bounding into your hostel room, humming a tune to herself that you couldn't quite place. You tried to find the melody in your memories, but Cherry was singing too fast, the notes were jumbled and strange.

'What's going on?' you said, throwing a clean top to her for packing.

She grabbed it and stuffed it into her suitcase. 'The guys next door asked us to go travelling around New Zealand with them.'

'Who next door?'

Cherry balled up a pair of socks and threw them into a bag. 'You *know*,' she said, a little breathless with excitement. 'Cameron, Ryan, Hanni. We were talking about it last night, remember?'

You shrugged. While you were in the room during this conversation – which was really more of a disorganised drinking game – you were not actually involved in it. You were planning bus and train routes, which took much longer than it should have done because the drunken hollering and beer-breath hugs kept distracting you.

Cherry sighed and crossed her arms. 'Why are you being so dismissive?'

'I'm not being dismissive.' You sighed back and tried to find words that wouldn't cause another argument. 'But we need to plan things like this. We can't just take off.'

'Why not? If we can't do it now, then when can we?'

'What about work? The rent? Where are we going to get the money from?' You looked down at the shirt in your hands, twisting it this way and that. 'I want to keep some savings aside for our future.'

'We'll get jobs here, then,' Cherry said, breezing past your reference to the future as if you'd said nothing. Her eyes were bright like Christmas lights.

You rubbed at your temples. 'And for that we'll need the right visa, a permanent address, and we'll need to give up our flat because we can't keep pay–'

'Don't talk to me like I'm a child!'

'I'm sorry, I didn't–'

'I'm going out.' She spun around and stormed out of the room, leaving the door open behind her.

'Cherry, wait!' you shouted after her. People in the corridor were trying not to stare. An eighteen-year-old student you'd met in the kitchen yesterday gave you a sympathetic smile, as if to say he knew exactly how you felt. You wished you could have stayed in a hotel, away from chipper young travellers and their overzealous friendliness. You pinched yourself hard on the arm. 'We need to leave early tomorrow. Where are you going?'

Cherry got back at three in the morning with lipstick smeared across her face. She climbed into bed and whispered, *I'm sorry, I'm sorry,'* into your back. You wanted to ask if she'd kissed someone else, but you held your tongue and let her hold you instead. She smelled like sweet perfume and other people's sweat.

'So, you're staying here?' you say now. The waves are getting taller, louder. The wind is whipping up the sand, scattering it everywhere. It takes everything in your lungs to make her hear you. 'That's it?'

You know the answer already. You know Cherry doesn't go with you, not really. Not with your food storage clips and your A3 wall calendar, your thirty-minute morning workouts and your quiet film nights with your two best friends (your only friends, really), your clean shoes and your hatred of mud and cold water and any logs that might have little creatures hiding underneath them. Cherry loves the outdoors. She loves the water. She can stand up on a surfboard now. She's not scared of big spiders or lizards or the bush turkeys that strut into your hostel like they own the place. She's good with strangers. People warm to her immediately. They tell her their life story; they remember her name. She even knows how to handle the fifty-something nuisance at your hostel who stands too close when he talks and finishes every sentence with, 'you understand?' *My wife studied for a long time to become a doctor, you understand? You add the milk gradually to the pan otherwise it will stick, you understand? It was the nineties, you understand? In Europe, you understand?*

You understand?

Cherry whirls around and stamps her foot down hard. 'I don't *know!*'

The waves rear up and crash into the beach, dragging away armfuls of sand for themselves. You raise your voice above them, letting your words fly out into the storm.

'What are you going to do, Cherry? You're going to stay here and – what?'

'I don't know! Stay here, travel around. I don't *know.*'

'What kind of plan is that?'

'Why have I got to have one? Why can't I just live?'

'So, you can't live when you're with me, is that it?'

Your hair is knotted with sand, your exposed skin is covered in sea spray. The papercut on your finger is stinging from the saltwater. How can a tiny wound hurt this much?

'*No!*' She throws the word out like a punch. 'It's always – we have work the next day, we need to fix the leak in the bathroom, we need to do the shopping list, we need to save money. It's exhausting.'

'Don't you shove that in my face,' you throw back. The wind changes direction, you brace yourself for impact as it hammers against your body. 'Those things are important.'

Cherry was a wreck before you got together. You rebuilt her. You took that upon yourself. You tried to right the wrongs of every arsehole she'd ever dated with good morning texts and cups of tea in bed and homemade lentil lasagne. You pieced her back together with trips to the pottery painting café and a regular alarm clock and daily walks even if it was pissing it down. You made her happy.

'You know we're different, we always have been,' Cherry says, her head tilted to one side like she thinks you understand what she's trying to say. *You understand?*

Cherry was never a relationship person. You knew that from the start. You found that exciting: that this person who'd been desired by so many others had chosen you. She could have had anyone she wanted, but it was you she went home with that night. The connection was immediate. You were used to dating app small talk and painfully awkward first dates that ended in teeth-bumping kisses and hollow promises to keep in touch. Everything was different with Cherry. She asked questions about your childhood and what you think happens when you die and whether you believe in a higher power or not. She talked about sex and her exes and poetry and politics. People like Cherry never chose you.

She said she wanted stability. You gave it to her. You would have given her anything.

'What are you saying, Cherry?' Your voice cracks. 'What are you saying?' you repeat, louder.

What was left of the daylight is fading. Black clouds are crawling across the sky, eclipsing the sun. The air is heavy, you feel the rain coming.

'I don't want to go home,' Cherry says, unblinking. Her voice is smooth and even despite the howling wind.

You press your palms to your chest, as if you might be able to hold your heart together with your hands. 'What about us, then?'

Cherry says nothing. She turns away, looks back towards the ocean.

You think about your life together, ten thousand miles away. The oval-shaped coffee table that Cherry found on Facebook Marketplace which you collected. The dented coffee machine that Cherry loves but never cleans. The fluffy turquoise rug on her side of the bed that you like to walk on barefoot. Your polished boots next to her scuffed trainers. The stiff window in the bathroom that only Cherry can open. Your Saturday morning walks to the café with the bad coffee and the good pastries that Cherry likes. The rare nights in watching nineties rom coms when for once, Cherry is too tired to go out. Those nights when you can finally hold her.

Cherry stands facing the sea, her chin tilted upwards towards the raging sky. Her eyes are closed, unbothered by the elements. Her long hair is dancing around her, reaching upwards, reaching away.

You understand, now, that she doesn't belong to you, that she never did belong to you. She is something different from you entirely, something you will never truly know. You understand, now, that you will never go back to that life with her, that it was never yours to have in the first place.

'I'm landing at Heathrow without you?' you say, knowing the question is pointless. The words feel strange leaving your mouth, like you are learning them for the first time. You cannot imagine arriving at Heathrow without her. You cannot imagine being in that place at all, cannot understand how it goes on existing, in the same way it always has, while you stand here on this ravaged beach watching your heart crack open.

Cherry turns around. You know her answer from her eyes.

Thunder ripples across the sky. Then the rain starts, drenching both of you within minutes. You walk away, leaving Cherry to the sea.

When you get home, you'll wonder if any of this really happened. Normal life will resume. You'll go back to your desk by the window and write articles about the green revolution and the presentation of masculinity in whatever comes after post-postmodern film. You'll tell your friends and family something about a mismatch of personalities, two people that wanted different things. You'll forget her, gradually, how she really was. She'll become an anecdote, something you talk about after one too many drinks, late at night with other people you won't love quite as much. You'll wonder, sometimes, what she did next, and if she ever thought about you. But all you'll have left is that memory of her, running away from you across that beach on the other side of the world.

Helen Kennedy

Helen Maire Kennedy is a Mancunian writer and playwright currently completing an MA in Creative Writing in Oxford. Her work, *Leaving Abhoca,* has been performed on stage by the Irish in London theatre (2019) and her short fiction and flash fiction has been shortlisted for the Cambridge prize, for the Flash Flood 2022 New Writers series, and her poetry published in the *Under the Sea* anthology by Fly on the Wall Press. She is currently working on her debut novel, *Blessed Women*, and a collection of flash fiction, *Manchester Fishing*.

We Are Now Approaching Wellingborough

The girl gets on the train at Corby and hasn't got a ticket. The guard says she'll have to get off at Wellingborough if she can't pay. He waits behind her as the train slows, as if to push her through the sliding doors and I say, 'Stop. I'll pay.' The girl stares at me, and the machine buzzes as the train manager issues a ticket. She holds it between her fingers, her hard bitten nails, red weals where the plastic bags have dug into them. She's wearing a headscarf, trousers underneath a long black skirt, a cardigan over a jumper and a thick coat; like she's wearing all her clothes at once. A fleece blanket is stuffed inside the carrier bag. The girl sits beside me, and I stare at my phone screen.

'Thank you,' she says.

The train slices between warehouses and builders yards, concrete walls and razor wire. A Poundland mega store off the ring road, with a smoking burger van in its carpark. The smell of the toilet as the carriage doors swish open. The girl checks and rechecks her phone. She is small under all those clothes, I think. She could be my daughter when she was eight.

'Do you know Victoria coach station?' the girl asks. Her voice is hard to tie down, Slavic maybe.

'Yes, it's a tube ride from St Pancras.'

'Can I walk there?'

'It's quite a distance. Better to get the tube,' I say and then back track. ' I can help with a ticket.' Underneath the sleeve of her cardigan, there are black hole burn marks on her wrists. I stare out of the window. Gravel pits and grey lakes, untethered ponies on land that looks partly submerged. Trees grow out of trees along the track here. 'Where are you going to?' I ask.

'Mtskheta, it's in Georgia,' she says. 'Home.'

'Gosh, that's a long way,' I say. The train pulls into Kettering and the man beside me drags his laptop case across me and for a moment he steps backwards as the train brakes, and I think he'll end up in my lap. Air is sucked out between carriages as the door opens and people get on and off. The rush of the automatic doors as they close tight.

'See it, say it. Sort it,' the announcement says, 'If you see anything suspicious contact British Transport Police.' There are gaps in my ability to acknowledge the present. Sometimes it's hard to recognise myself. The tea trolley rumbles by and the man in blue uniform pumps hot water into a polystyrene cup.

'Would you like a tea?' I ask. The girl shakes her head and produces another phone from underneath her clothing, it must have been lodged inside her bra, I think. It's one of those cheap black mobiles, now dead and she asks to plug it into the socket beside me.

'I have a daughter,' I say. Her phone springs to life, the light up screen buzzes and tings new messages. 'She doesn't live with me, she's at uni.' I don't know why I've said that and spill my coffee. The couple in the double seat beside me share a look.

The train rocks and drones as we pick up speed. Alongside the track is scrubby wasteland, embankments slip away into fields and hedges. A disordered landscape.

'I wanted to go to university,' the girl says. 'I wanted to be a teacher, so I moved to Tbilisi, to work in a bar and earn some money.'

Hoodie man opposite me yawns and stretches, and I can see the back of his throat. He kicks my leg accidentally but pretends he hasn't. The guard brings a bin bag to collect the rubbish and the girl throws in the phone, the one with the pink unicorn phone case and I stare at her.

'It's not mine,' she says. 'Someone gave it to me.' Her wrists are thin like bones, and I want to hold them.

At Luton Airport Parkway people get on and off with wheelie cases and crowd around us. The smell of new air.

'There is no train to my town, the bus it takes seven hours,' the girl says. Her face is perfectly still. 'I haven't seen my mother in a long time.'

The woman with pointed shoes wrestles her bag into the overhead storage. She's a smoker, her gold puffa jacket reeks of it. Fences and back gardens, sky dishes and solar panelled roofs, new houses on muddy building sites. Old trees with thick bark and broken branches. The train is all electric, but it still smells like diesel.

'My daughter's in Brighton,' I say. 'She writes poetry.' Her phone buzzes to life and she's got seventeen messages but doesn't read them. Sometimes we don't want to see it or sort it. I think about the rim of pebbled beach, the tide breathing in and out, and the smell of candyfloss. Hove on the horizon; a place we can't seem to reach. Her promise.

'Off Peak tickets are not accepted on this service,' the train announcer says. A man wearing a suit gets on at Bedford and spreads his legs wide, his tight trousers over thick thighs and the girl holds her plastic bag to her chest. Underneath her layers she is breathing hard. A seat for two people comes free and I nudge the girl and we move on to it together.

'Are you going to work,' she says.

'No, I'm going to the theatre, to see a play called Cyrano de Bergerac. James McAvoy's in it, do you know him? He was Mr Tumnus.' She nods but she doesn't know what I'm talking about. I look away, breathe slowly through my hands. I'll be able to sit in the dark for a few hours, pretend to be someone else.

After Luton, the train squeezes between steep inclines. The embankment full of McDonald's cardboard boxes and cups with straws. I offer the girl an Eccles cake from my bag. And I think about my daughter being five and calling them dead fly cakes, licking the sugar off them and learning to love them years later when her boyfriend's mum baked them. Nothing is ever what it seems.

I stare out of the greasy window. The drone of the M1 as the train races three lanes of motorway traffic. London Gateway services pump steam into the sky. It's three years since you left home.

'I've been working in a nail bar,' the girl says. 'shit money.'

It must have been last Christmas that I bought baby milk for a Big Issue seller in Stamford. A girl with thin lips and pale skin who sat on a cushion outside Costa Coffee. I offered to buy her a latte, but she said that she really needed milk for her baby. When I put the tin of SMA Follow-On Milk by her feet, a man in a hoodie came over and said she'd prefer cash. She looked at me for a moment but didn't speak. I bought her a coffee but when I came out, she had gone.

The girl reaches out to touch my hand. She doesn't need to say anything. I close my eyes.

'Nish' is written in neon paint on hoardings, and I imagine that 'Nish' is probably a guy in a snap back and high tops, with chunky gold rings. Heavy washing hangs from plastic rope strung across a yard, a man sits and smokes on his back doorstep, black tunnels and silence.

A year ago, I wandered North Laines, among the arty street people, vintage sellers and Trading Post coffee shops. I thought that someone must know the girl with the blue hair, an elbow thin bohemian, called Mia. A beautiful soul. When I knocked on the metal door at Kings Mansions, a guy called Bray in a sheepskin coat said he'd tell you I called. Afterwards I sat on the promenade and stared up into the lighted window and imagined that you were inside drinking coffee and making chermoula for dinner. He texts me from time to time, to say you're doing ok. A relay of sorts, passing on words from one person to another. I like to think that you ask him to text me. I imagine that you spend your days on the beach, dipping into the sea, watching the waves crash, with the sun on your face. A sort of tragicomedy.

The girl's phone keeps ringing, so she turns it off and turns away.

'The next stop is London St Pancras,' the rail voice says. Lines of wires hang between wooden telegraph poles. The train disappears and reappears through bridges with oversized graffiti, railings, miles of steel with spikes, haulage yards and truck stops. Urban dog walkers on wet pavements. What we see from the railway is always life back to front. Hidden. It's what life is really like behind the scenes.

It's my mother's birthday,' the girl says. 'I want to take her flowers. I smile and think about roses and tulips and the scent of spring flowers.

'Your phone – it just rang,' the girl says.

I listen to the voice message. *Please ring Dr Christopher Eames urgently.*' There is a text message from Bray that says, '*A&E Royal Sussex Hospital*,' and I know that my life will be split open from this point. No return journey and I should have done more.

The train is plunged into darkness. The longest tunnel.

I remember having our fortunes told on West Pier, Madame Zelda turning over my palms and telling me that there was a break in my heart line. That you would travel and try many new things in life before you settled somewhere. Afterwards we ate chips and said it was a load of bullshit.

'Are you ok?' the girl asks, and I realise that she's holding her small hands around mine. The flashlight of London skyline, West Hampstead station, blue central sky. We approach the arc of St Pancras station, the steel and glass curve of apartments. The Javelin train leans into the track beside us. Hanson cement pumps smoke and stands tall. The train creaks and slows to a stop.

At the barriers, I fumble in my pocket for my ticket to post into the machine. It always makes me anxious and unprepared. The girl is weighted with her plastic bags, balanced one in each hand and is already disappearing into the crowd on the other side. The man in the beanie hat, and white Puma tracksuit waits by the escalator. He puts his hand on the girl's neck. She doesn't look back.

In the women's toilets we pass each other in the queue, and she smiles. Her mouth is small and precious.

'I'm not following you,' I say. But I take a pen from my bag and write my phone number on the back of her hand and say, 'I'm Helen.'

'It's not what you think,' she says. It never is.

Elen Lewis

Elen Lewis is a writer and English teacher. Following a career as a ghostwriter, when she wrote 20 books she can't talk about, Elen now teaches at Turing House, a state secondary school. Elen's poetry has been exhibited at The Welsh National Eisteddfod, The Story Museum and London's V&A. Elen was born in Llangollen in the foothills of Snowdonia and studied English at Oxford University. Elen lives with her husband, two children and a dog called Bee, in London.

Lightning Girl

Ionawr (January)

None of us took much notice of Beth Llewellyn until she was struck by lightning.

It was less of a light and more of a flame lick, she told us. A sort of a crackling jolty lift.

At first, some of us thought she'd made it up. But then lightning flowers started growing up her arms. It was as if she was turned inside out.

Chwefror (February)

The sky is clabbered and the sheep stand still.

The lightning strikes the field over and over and when we run there afterwards, we can dig the potatoes out of the ground, still warm and eat them all yellow powdery and soft.

Beth gathers some into the folds of her skirt and carries them home.

Mawrth (March)

Beth has taken to climbing Velvet Mountain when dawn cracks like egg yolk across the sky. People see her talking to herself and we wonder if she's praying or has lost her mind.

The boys flit around like moths to a flame, asking her to lift her top so they can see the scars on her back. She blushes and shows them.

At dusk when the air is milky, the butcher's boy, Sam, takes Beth on a long walk along the ridge. We see them kissing by the far gate. We wait a long time behind curtains for their return.

Ebrill (April)
We can't stop looking at the sky. We gather in clumps on the field and watch the lightning chalk up the night.

All the gossip in the village is about Beth. If anyone asked us why there were more storms this year, we could not answer.

Come on Beth, we say. Show us how you call the lightning. It's not like that, says Beth. It's not like that at all.

Mai (May)
Clouds race over the mountains bumping into things.

I hovered above you all, says Beth. The world slowed down and I could see into the next valley all the way to the sea.

We roll our eyes at her boasting. Our washing swells and flaps in the wind like a sail.

Some of us think that if one lightning strike is pure bad luck, two is witchcraft. We cross the road when we see her coming with her yellow eyes and her raspy voice.

There was so much light, she says to anyone still listening. So much light.

Sam says Beth's lightning flowers have blistered into angry burns. He says they look ugly.

She is very alone in the world.

Mehefin (June)
It doesn't take long for the Lightning Seekers to discover our valley of thunder and lightning. They come wearing strange clothes, galoshes that reach their thighs and hats with brims as wide as parasols.

Gorffennaf (July)
The light disappears earlier than it used to. We think it's because the sun is exhausted. The swollen river roars. Dogs bark. Crows craw.

The mayor from the next village comes with a party over the pass. He's heard tales of a yellow-eyed girl churning up the skies and sucking visitors from all over like water through a straw.

He marches up and down in front of her and looks at her from all angles. He offers her a woodland cottage with an apple tree.

We can't decide if we want her to leave or stay around. Some of us are fed up with the whole business.

I can't switch it off like a tap, says Beth. I can't just decide there's no more lightning.

She yawns and stretches in the gloam. She is as pale as milk.

Awst (August)
When the storms blow away, the ants fly in. The river shrinks to a stream and at night we cannot sleep.

Somebody is leaving origami swans on our doorsteps like peace offerings and we believe it might be Beth.

We are restless, lighting fires in the woods, teasing dogs, killing spiders. At night we bolt the doors.

Medi (September)
A murmuration of starlings peck a swan to death and it lies on the rocks like a question mark.

It spoke to me, says Beth. I heard its swan song. We roll our eyes and walk away.

A shoal of dead fish wash up in the weir.

Next day, chapel is rammed to the rafters.

Hydref (October)
The sky is black as coal and the thunder rumbles inside the valley making dogs howl and sheep scatter.

Lightning fells a herd of cows, bleaching them white. The earth smells of scorched flesh. I don't think it was me, says Beth. You know I wouldn't hurt them on purpose.

But we don't believe her.

We fear that we're being sent a message from above. We just wish we knew what it was.

Tachwedd (November)
The sky smashes into the mountains. The rain falls like exclamation marks. We open our mouths and taste it on our tongues.

We watch Beth hang in the clouds like a make-believe bird in a make-believe sky.

We are very tiny things in the universe. We think that we have never seen such fine beauty as when the rain falls down so strong and sad on our valley flooding our heads with rhythm.

Rhagfyr (December)
We wonder if Beth thinks of us. We wonder if she's looking down at the pigs near the barn and the thick, green moss clinging onto the rocks. We wonder if she knows she ruined our valley. We think about her all the time. And it's a strange kind of longing. We miss her and we don't miss her. We watch the sky and wait for a storm. We know we'll never see lightning again.

Ananya Mahapatra

Ananya Mahapatra is an Indian writer. Her short stories and writings have been published in *Plethora Blogazine, Women's Web, Kitaab International,* and *Hektoen International.* Her short story, *Confessions of a Neurotypical Mom* was published in *Twilight's Children,* a collection of stories on disability, by the Indian publishing house Readomania. Her short story *The Bureaucrat's Wife* was amongst the twenty stories shortlisted for the *Best Asian Short Stories Anthology 2019,* published by Kitaab International, Singapore. She is also a psychiatrist, practising in New Delhi, and is currently working on a collection of short stories based on the lives and longings of people in her home city. She is also the founder of a literary wellness blog thelifesublime.org – a labour of love to bring together her vocation and her love for writing.

Naanwai

I cannot put my finger on the exact moment, when his shop became for me, an island of solace – even though it stands at the far end of Masjid Lane, in one of the busiest corners of the marketplace. It is barely a one-room structure. There are squatter shacks like that all over the city – built by simply piling one brick on top of another, with nothing more than a tentative layer of cement between them, the bricks covered with thin blue paint, without plastering underneath. There is an old *Amaltas* tree leaning on its left wall with long, drooping branches that arch over the asbestos roof, covering it with a canopy of yellow blossoms. Inside, a huge clay oven takes up most of the space.

A few wooden benches are spread out in the front, the fading yellow paint on them falling off in slivers. They are the kind you see in primary schools run by the Delhi Government, for those who cannot afford private education. If he had children, they would be studying in one of these schools. Provided he had the right kind of documents, of course – not just the little blue paper that doesn't get you anywhere. But his children have probably grown up and are far away. The wide curve of his brows is peppered with grey, and the caverns of his cheeks are covered in a scruffy white beard.

He lives on his own, in his shop, which is also his home. I know this because I have seen him sleep, curled up beside the big coal oven.

It must keep the floor warm during winters, but I wonder how he survives the incinerating heat of the summers in this city. The narrow counter at the front side appears to have been fashioned out of a broken benchtop. From daybreak, till the fading light of dusk, he stands behind this counter, his face obscured by mounds of dough and a varied assortment of bread.

A vinyl board hung over his head with only one word written in cheap white paint: *Naanwai*

***

The word is written in English, even though it is not an English word or a Hindi one for that matter. For those who are from here, it rolls off their tongues hesitantly. It's a word they are not familiar with. But it doesn't matter. The pile of bread – large, flaky, and foreign-looking – and the steaming vat of tea are enough to tell them what he is selling.

But the alley where his shop stood was also home to those who were from elsewhere. They, like him, have built their lives around the close-packed tenements that lined this busy road. To them, the word made sense, perhaps, in more ways than one. Sometimes, I wonder if it carried with it, whispers of the cities they arrived from, the silence of those left behind – whether the spaces between its syllables are wide enough to contain the remnants of an aftermath. I am not from here, or a place that far away. The murmurs of my past are not bloodied by gunshots, but there are other kinds of violence as well.

Naanwai for me is a name: the only one by which I know him.

***

Every evening, I walk up to his end of the street, without breaking stride. I sit on one of the benches littered with pigeon droppings and yellow *Amaltas* flowers. I am the only woman there.

On most days, I am on my own. From morning till evening, people buy their bread and leave. *Naanwai* hands them over in coarse brown bags. His rates are dirt cheap: twenty rupees for a loaf; ten rupees for a cup of tea. His customers are mostly other Afghan refugees like him. I catch fragments of *Dari* or *Pashto*; I can't tell the difference. The sibilant notes of their exchange soothe my frazzled nerves, and I listen, even though I don't understand a word.

Men and women flock mostly to the new restaurants – with Middle Eastern decor and flashy names – that have mushroomed near the main Bhogal Road. In the evening, their interiors glow with pink strobe lights, and notes of Arabic trance waft in the air. They are a hit with the young Delhi crowd who come here for doner kebabs, shawarma rolls, Kabuli pilaf, and traditional lamb chops. To keep up with the times, these places now offer modern renditions: *afghani tikka, afghani chaap, afghani burger, afghani pizza...* Whatever you seek, you shall get in a new-fangled *afghani* version.

After business is done, *Naanwai* kneads his dough under the harsh glow of an LED tube. It takes a whole night for the flour to rise. I know this because sometimes I linger even after his last loaf of the day is sold. On some days he plays music on a pocket-size transistor. Every time, the muffled voice of a man – who I know now is called Sarban – sings the same song. The music is sombre, symphonic like an anthem. I now recognize the soft refrain: *Ahesta boro...* It's a song they play for brides on their wedding day.

His shop is not shuttered like the rest. Every evening he pulls down a sheet of tarpaulin, repurposed to shelter him from heat, cold, and rain, and to protect his dough from marauding strays. It shines like a bat's wings in the folds of which he recedes for the night. On many days, it signals the moment when I retrace my steps back to my room.

***

I live in Bhogal, minutes away from Masjid Lane, only because the rent is affordable. That the tight community of this locality housed people, who long before me drifted here from other places they called home, is an irony I find fortuitous. I too, came here seeking sanctuary, even if my troubles weren't as momentous as the Partition. But like those who came before me, I know how sometimes safe harbours splinter at the bottom and cast you into treacherous waters.

I double-check the bolts on my door when I get back. At night, I dream of lightning blazing through the spine of a tree. Halfway through I realize it's not a tree. I see myself standing right where the tree was supposed to be. I see a flash, a filigree of burns blooming, and angry red rivers charting their course on my skin. I wake up to the ragged beating of my heart, drenched in a cold sweat, my *kurta* clinging to my back. I count the hours till dawn that I will now pass sleeplessly. But I fall asleep eventually, a whisker away from sunrise, and wake up again near noon to a dull ache in my chest, the last dregs of the terror that seized the night.

***

The first time I was at the shop, *Naanwai* came to me with a slice of *roht* and a cup of tea.

He did not offer me a choice, even though there were other options:

large fluffy discs of *khameeri, bolani* stuffed with spiced vegetables; wafer-thin *lavasas* I have seen women buy in dozens.

Roht is a sweet bread infused with the scent of cardamom. It is peppered with nigella seeds on top and its surface is brushed with butter. I bite into the soft warm bread and sense something unfastening within me. As if a tumbled piece of stone stuck in my throat, had finally been unstuck.

***

The memories of last year are curdled in my mind. Fragments of time congealed – like clotted blood – into a scab I kept picking at, drawing blood.

It all began with a slow procession around a ceremonial fire. He walked with a subtle limp on the left side. I noticed that on the first day when there was still some distance between us. Soon that space was squeezed shut so that his shoulders now brushed forcefully against mine. His fingers clamped around my waist, not jauntily, but with the quiet certitude of a man in possession of something he owns. I see myself from a distance once again, and I see the walls closing in, even though I did not see them then.

The only good thing I remember from this past is the garden. It was a little patch of land in the backyard of the house we moved in. There was a time when he looked pleased to see his new wife emerge from a thicket of peonies, sweaty-browed, arms soiled up to her elbows. But even then, there were signs – the way he wrenched the lantanas off their stalks and stuffed them haphazardly into empty bottles. He said the purpose of the flowers was to make the house look pretty. Soon enough the dark moods descended on him, and he said flowers served no purpose at all. Why couldn't I grow vegetables instead? Tomatoes, sweet peas, celery, cilantro, and aubergines – that are fresh and homegrown, not the pesticide-riddled garbage you buy from the market these days.

Now that you must stay at home, why don't you make yourself useful? I remember the way he mouthed the words "*must*" and "*useful*". I worked at a pharmacy store before the wedding. But I didn't remind him of that. Most of the days, I didn't say anything. I was learning the art of circumvention. It begins with silence.

Those days are gone now, but times have ways to sneak back into your life. You must keep the doors bolted – at all times.

***

Naanwai tells me his home is in a village close to a town called *Mazar-i-Sharif*, and that he has not stepped on its soil for one whole year now. I do not ask him why – why he had to leave, who he had to leave behind. He speaks Hindi in a soft deliberate way and makes the language his own. We tell each other little things, now that I am at the shop almost every day. I ask him if he thinks of this as an aberration.

It is not unusual for women to visit him, he tells me, with a smile. In his village, women do not bake bread at home. It's a morning ritual, to make a trip to the nearest *Naanwai* for bread that will last for a day. Smoke pluming from his chimney signals dawn; the smell of his baking holds promises of bellies warm and full. Yes, they do not stay for long, though. A kitchen is never without work, and children are always famished. The women come in clusters; they grab their loaves and hurry back home. There is always so much to do...

He is rattling on with infectious energy when he stops suddenly. I am conscious of his gaze, his mineral-green eyes, the color of ocean beds. His look is intent, not probing. I do not tell him why I am at his shop almost every evening; why I stay on, even after the sun has disappeared behind a jagged skyline; why I sit on a bench and eat sweet bread on my own, instead of taking it back home. The contours of our stories do not matter now that we can read the silence that ebbs and flows between us.

His face is a cartographer's canvas. The lines on his forehead, his eyelids, the bridge of his nose, and the curve of his jaw, map the terrain through which long and perilous journeys have been undertaken. There are fleeting moments when the light comes alive in his eyes, when he talks of his desert village and what life is like under its limitless blue sky. But those moments are rare. They pass, and a window is again shuttered, blurring the lineaments of the past. A curtain falls, like the tarpaulin cover, behind which he disappears every night. At that moment he becomes again – a bread seller on a crowded city street in a foreign country.

Later that night, I lie on my bed in my room, and I search for *Mazar-i-Sharif* on my phone. A towering mosque with a spectacular blue dome fills my screen. I stare for a long time at the tranquility of its long marble corridors, until I fall asleep. I do not dream of lightning searing my flesh, after many, many nights.

***

I started growing vegetables the way he wanted me to. The patch had not been tended for long. In the hours when he was gone, I raked the dead leaves. I pulled out the weeds. I trimmed the errant branches of the shrubs that lined its perimeter. The summer heat had petrified the soil into hard clumps. I poured big pails of water, till the earth loosened up to let air and moisture seep into its layers. In a month, tomato vines creeped out to seek the sun. Large leafy spinach sprouted, and cauliflower florets cropped in little clusters. The silent work of nature filled me with hope. *Can verdure soften a man's heart?*

He complained that I was spending too much time in the garden. On his way back, if he saw me working, dark clouds gathered on his face. I saw his eyes ablaze with thundering rage. Some days he said nothing. On other days, he stomped on the lettuce and coriander sprigs on his way inside. He decapitated cauliflower crowns with his boot.

At dinner, he pointed with disgust at the mud that congealed under my nails, even when there was none. He discovered specks of dirt cunningly interred in the webs between my fingers. He complained the food tasted of loam, that we might as well live in a compost pit. I tiptoed around his wrath and his unreason, whenever I could. During one of his fits, he scrubbed my fingers with a vehemence so vicious, that it made my nail beds bleed. After that, I gave up the garden altogether.

But his tempers continued to soar at unpredictable moments, over occurrences so trivial that it was impossible to sense their coming. But I learned to take notes: *dripping faucets, mist on the mirrors; soap bubbles on the washbasin; a crease in the curtains, crumbs on the bedclothes.* Every new item on the list made my skin eloquent with cautionary symbols – blue-green patches on my back; purple ones on my shin; crimson streaks on my cheekbones. The relics of my learning nursed a lasting ache in my ribs, that flares unexpectedly even now.

And on one such evening of malice and rage, when I crouched on the cold wet earth of my garden to soothe the throbbing at the root of my spine, where he had brought down his boot to drive home his education, it dawned on me: *if I wanted to live, I had to get away from this place that was meant to be my home.*

***

For the first time, I find the shop closed, the black tarpaulin cover pulled down at half-past four in the evening. I panic for a second. *Is he gone?*

I do not know, how it came into being, or why I keep coming back to this place, but ever since I had left home, this sojourn has become the ritual of a new life I was trying to ease into. I sit on a bench under the tree and wonder if *Naanwai* would be here later in the evening, tomorrow, ever. For one drastic moment, I think he had gone back to his village, but it did not make sense. If the act of fleeing home is a long and onerous enterprise, the act of reclaiming it is a near-impossible one. I think of going back to the house with the garden, and fear turns my marrow into stone. There are more merciful ways to perish.

***

I come back the next day to find the shop running as usual, and *Naanwai* behind his benchtop counter. His brows are furrowed, and he shovels coal into the oven absently, barely looking up at his customers.

I touch his wrist when he hands me my cup of tea. If it surprised him, he doesn't let it show. He doesn't even turn to look in my direction. but after he has served those waiting at the counter, he wipes the flour off his hands and sits next to me on the bench, his shoulders hunched in a way that makes him look suddenly small, despite his towering frame.

Troubles have escalated in his hometown and everywhere else.

I had seen the news on TV – the video clippings of American aircraft airlifting troops and paramedics playing on a loop, while diplomats and experts on foreign affairs mulled over America's next big move, now that the Taliban are steadily gaining ground, and the national government is down on its knees.

He tells me he has been saving money to bring his daughter here. She has a daughter of her own, born last summer, two months after her husband was taken. His voice glazed with a fear that was new even to me. His son-in-law, who worked for the government, was ambushed one night by men in black robes. That was the last time they saw him. They did not find his body. She wouldn't believe he was dead, even though the black robes were homing in everywhere, executing men and women in the dead of the night. She will join him once she has her answers – she told him the night he went away. Since then, he has been waiting, sending her money, begging her to gather the strength to let go, to make a safe passage while there was still time.

***

I wake up to drum rolls and a marching band.

It's the fifteenth of August, and the children of a primary school two blocks away are celebrating Independence Day. I hear our national anthem in a high-pitched, off-key chorus and instinctively stand up. For the minute when the anthem is playing, I feel I am one with them, these primary school pupils who are singing of their freedom, our freedom. They will go home once the ceremony is over, with a packet of *laddoos*, waving little tricolour paper flags of their own.

It's a national holiday. The market is closed. The TV channels have a list of patriotic Bollywood movies lined up for the day. I turn on the news channel without any discernible purpose, and the animated voice of a newsreader fills my room. She is talking to a special correspondent who had just flown in from Kabul. A grainy footage plays out in the background where I see the men in black robes storming a city, chanting slogans, their rifles raised to the sky. *The President has left the country*, she informed me in an ominous tone. *The American troops are heading back home.* I see people huddled like sheep on rocky roads. They walk in files to border towns. It looks like a march of pilgrims seeking deliverance.

How far will you go when home is not home anymore?

I wonder if there is an antonym for *independence*. And since the loss of liberty is no less momentous than achieving it, shouldn't there be a day etched in history, in remembrance of its loss? My thoughts turned to *Naanwai*'s daughter. I wonder if she was somewhere in the faceless crowds, walking away like the others, or is she still holding her ground, looking for a husband who was taken? How terrible is the price that you pay for averting your gaze when danger is closing in on you? For not getting away while you can?

I think of the garden I had left behind — lonely, slowly turning barren, now that it is bereft of care, once again. I see sweet pea tendrils shrivelling in the heat; tomato vines wilting without water. I see weeds taking over my cabbage beds; the green grass turning yellow, then brown, the soft wet earth hardening once more under a menacing sun. And I see boots — dark-coloured, cattle hide rough-side-out — stomping out signs of newly sprouted life.

I reel with a sudden bout of agitation, as I get up abruptly to unlock the double bolts on my door. It's only eleven in the morning, but I know where I have to be.

***

The stretch from my room to the shop is unusually desolate this morning.

Most shops have their shutters down. The caterwaul of bargaining customers is absent, the snarl of traffic subdued. I only hear snatches of patriotic songs playing out from distant loudspeakers. I walk through a warren of narrow lanes, crisscrossing the entire breadth of the market; the streets, usually bustling with thoroughfare, are empty.

The lane on which my apartment building stood, meets a bifurcation of roads, one of which leads me to *Naanwai*'s shop. At that point, against the high wall of a building, I see a shadow – sharp, angular, and leaning leftwards. It is the shadow of a man, moving, limping, slowly in my direction. I cannot see his face, but his gait has a staccato rhythm I recognize – like when the right foot moves forward, and the left one must drag itself to keep up.

My legs are turning into lead, and flames run through my insides. I am ambushed by a terror that is not new. *What we flee from never truly leaves us.* They cast pale shadows on our backs; they bide their time. Time will look you in the eye and turn everything around its axis. It will make the past present and the present past. All you get is a split second – to look away, to turn your back, and run. I don't know for how long I kept running, but when I reached the shop, a fire was burning in my back. I collapsed on a bench – gasping for air as cold dread closed its fingers around my throat.

Naanwai is there, as usual, flattening portions of dough into bread shapes. I cannot tell if he had seen the news – the fleet of black-robed men shrouding his home in darkness – but when he looks at me, I see the fear in my bones turning his green eyes, grey.

Naanwai steps away from his counter. He takes my hand with a tenderness that makes me want to double down, like a leaf in a storm, and weep. He moves aside and steers me to his one-room shack, his only refuge. He beckons me, almost prods me inside. The room is dark, like an alcove, but warm, and I can barely make out his outline as he steps back outside, leaving me on my own in this room, engulfed in shadows, where the oven casts an orange glow on the walls.

It is a ridiculously tiny room, but at this moment, it's a fortress – its blue brick walls are the only thing that stands between me and the advancing edge of darkness. I kneel on the floor, beside the oven, alive with its slow-burning flame, as the tarpaulin sheet rolls down like an iron veil to hide me from this world.

David Micklem

David Micklem is a writer and theatre producer. His first novel, *The Winter Son*, is currently on submission through his agent Robert Caskie. In the last year he's been published by STORGY Magazine, *The Cardiff Review, Lunate*, Bandit Fiction and TigerShark Publishing, and was shortlisted for the Fish Short Story Prize and longlisted for the Brick Lane Bookshop and SaveAs International Short Story Prizes. He lives in Brixton, South London.

Girls and Boys

Back then, Jack was a boy. He was two years above me, and our sisters were pals. I knew him to say hi to and Jack said my mum took us all to see Toy Story 3 when we were about ten years old, but I don't remember him coming. If you asked me then I would have said he was a bit of a loser, a bit up himself, maybe. They lived in one of the smart houses on Bay View Road and that was probably the main reason why I didn't like him much in those days.

After Da left we moved into the ugliest bungalow on Frairshill. It looked like something a kid who couldn't draw might come up with. If I close my eyes, I can see its two big windows staring at me disapprovingly. Ma and my sister still live there. Last summer they painted the front door pink and I told them it looks like a tongue in the photograph they sent.

I wasn't good at school and me and my mate Rory spent all of our time riding motorbikes up past the rugby club and then along the coast road to Clonmannon. I got good at fixing them up and I think Ma spotted that and stopped giving me such a hard time about my studies. She thought I might become a mechanic, do stuff with my hands, but I wanted to race bikes or be in a band.

Friday nights Rory and I would be off into town. Ma would try and stop me, saying it was dangerous on the coast road, in the dark. But we were fearless and rode as fast as we could, side by side roaring through all the towns and villages like we didn't give a shit what anybody thought.

Rory was seventeen too but looked older and had no trouble getting us served in the pubs. I had bum fluff on my top lip and I used my sister's mascara to make it look like a proper moustache. We didn't have much money, but we got good at nicking other peoples' drinks when they weren't looking. We'd down a couple of pints and watch a band and then race back on the bikes before my Ma got too anxious or started ringing the hospital.

There would have been six weeks between the end of the exams and getting my results. It was obvious that I was going to fail them all. I'm not an idiot but I just didn't see the point in all that hard work when I had a bike and a few Euro in my pocket. That summer was like something out of a film. Long hot days and short nights with girls and drink and not a care in the world. I bleached my hair and I thought I looked like Ryan Gosling until I'd catch my reflection and the soft breath of disappointment at my image.

Me and Rory and a whole bunch of us would head over to Leamore Strand and hang out in the dunes and go swimming. If I think back now it seems like every day was bright and sunny and that that's all we did but I know enough to know that memories are strange things, twisted and uneven, never quite what they seem.

I started work at the butchers in town and I never had anything to complain about. My sister told me that Aoife Gallagher had a crush on me and I took her on the back of my bike out to the woods beyond the golf course and she let me touch her the first time I asked. I used a rubber like Rory had told me and after a week I said I didn't fancy her anymore and she started seeing Eoin Stephenson.

It was that summer that we got really into The Photons. They played Fridays at The Palace Bar and Rory knew the drummer's brother, so we got to hang out with them sometimes after a gig.

One weekend after The Palace there was a party in this old warehouse just over the river and by the time Rory and I got there we knew we weren't heading back to Wicklow that night. I had this heavy chain that I wore like a belt and used it to lock the bikes to each other and a lamppost just off O'Connell Bridge.

Inside the party was like a nightclub. Lights and lasers and Paul who played keyboards with the band was DJing. Rory's mate had told us to bring booze and we turned up with a plastic bag full of cans and a bottle of Bushmills. The room was huge and at one end there was a raised area with beds and sofas on it, and beneath that a kitchen where someone had set up a table for the drinks.

We made our way slowly across to the bar and Rory kept saying 'be cool, be cool' out of the side of his mouth, his teeth gritted.

We put the cans on the table, took one each, and stashed the Bushmills behind a sofa. I stood in the far corner while Rory went to find his mate. A steady flow of partygoers filled the place and I tried to look casual, like I couldn't really be arsed with any of it. I was leaning on some old piece of industrial equipment when this fella came up to me and asked for a smoke.

"Cheers," he said, snapping his Zippo shut, offering me his hand. "Paulie."

He told me he was a music journalist and a fan of The Photons, and we got talking about the gig and the new single 'Girls and Boys'. I reckoned he might be eighteen, and that he was bullshitting about being a journalist, but he knew his stuff about the band and when Rory came back we chatted about other music we liked.

Parties in Wicklow were pretty lame affairs by comparison. There'd always be someone who'd drunk too much, too quick. It was Richie Reynolds, usually. He loved the drink, and someone was always having to keep an eye on him when he hurled in the bathroom or passed out on the stairs.

The warehouse party was like nothing I'd been to before. All these cool kids with great haircuts and fantastic boots. Art school, Rory reckoned, and later on I found myself sandwiched on a sofa between the Photons' drummer and a guy who had a snake tattoo that wrapped itself right around his neck. We passed the whisky back and forth and drank straight from the bottle and then this girl plonked herself on my lap without even asking.

"Kelly," she said, ruffling my hair and, although I knew I needed to be cool, I think I just stared at her.

She grabbed the bottle from the guy with the tattoo, took a gulp and then kissed me on the lips. Her mouth was hot and smoky, and I felt dizzy, unable to move.

"Hey…" I said, pretending I wasn't interested which was weird because I really was.

Kelly was American and had pink and black shoulder length hair and dark blue makeup on her eyelids so that when she blinked it looked like her eyes were still open. She was from California and even though I was pretty drunk I tried hard not to show too much interest. There were hundreds of people at the party and I couldn't see why she'd picked on me, some guy with a bad dye job and bum fluff from Wicklow. I half-expected a roar of laughter when the joke was revealed, the dare exposed.

Kelly asked if I wanted to go for a smoke and when Rory heard and looked at me with buggy eyes, I told him to 'be cool, be cool' and sauntered off to the loading doors that opened out onto a yard.

I felt like I was watching me and Kelly from above, like we were being filmed. It was thrilling and I didn't know my lines, my next move, and I didn't care. I was torn – between wanting to tell her I was seventeen, that I'd never been to a party like this before, that my Ma would be worrying – and acting like this was just like every other Friday night. I had to hold on to the frame of the door but a part of me just wanted to let go, to fall.

"You ok, hon?" she asked, stubbing out her cigarette and taking my hand.

It was like she could read my mind and I smiled, weakly. I wanted Kelly to tell me what to do, how to be.

"C'mon. Let's get some air."

She led me out through the crowd, and it was like a spotlight followed us all the way. On the street it was still and quiet and the lights were orange like tiny suns. She swung my arm and skipped, and we made our way down the street and back to O'Connell Bridge. I felt like we were being watched but there was no one else around.

"Here," I said, pointing at the bikes, and she giggled and swung her leg over, grabbing the handlebars.

"You look good on there."

"Jump on!" she said, and I sat behind her, wrapping my arms around her waist.

She smelt of soap and smoke and I leaned my head against her back, and she made the noise of the motorbike, twisting the throttle, her arms bent.

I closed my eyes and held her tight and tried hard not to cry. It must have been the booze because I should have been happy. She was gorgeous and American, and it was just the two of us, a warm breeze and the lights sparkling off the river. But there was something in my throat and I wished my Da hadn't run away, and that this moment, just me and Kelly, would never end.

She stopped making the noise of the bike and leaned back and I held her, my nose buried in her hair, her neck. She didn't say anything, and I think she knew that I was fine and I didn't want it to end, the ride. She rocked gently in my arms, and we stayed like this for ages.

I imagined riding down a road lined with palm trees all the way to the ocean. She was so confident with everything, like she knew exactly what she was doing. Her voice all growly like it was full of smoke. For a while she hummed gently and, without looking, I knew she had her eyes shut. It was lovely, just the two of us, and I held her like a gift. I felt if I let go, she might take it away for ever.

I thought about my Da and wondered where he was right now. I remembered how he'd take me to the chipper on Friday nights on the back of his moped and we'd eat them down on the front staring out across the sea. He told me once about a girlfriend he'd had in Bristol, and I wondered if that's where he'd gone and whether he thought about me now.

My Ma would be. Sitting at home, watching some bollocks on the TV, starting to worry.

And then I thought about my sister and Rory, and Aoife Gallagher and all my mates in Wicklow. And Kelly in my arms, like a story no one would ever believe. We stayed like this until her legs went numb and it felt like we'd ridden all the way to California.

"Hey," she said, and we turned together to sit side-saddle and face out along the river.

I felt for her hand, and she squeezed my fingers.

"I think I love you Kelly," I said, and I think I was more surprised than she was to hear those words out in the world.

"You're very sweet. And much too young to be falling in love with someone like me. Your friend'll be trying to figure what happened to the two of us. C'mon."

She grabbed my hand and we were back at the party before I'd had a chance to think, to be properly heartbroken. I didn't think I knew about love between a boy and a girl until that night. And then there it was, something hot and heavy in my chest, like a baked potato, and I didn't know if it was Kelly or thinking about my Da or Wicklow or just the Bushmills.

She disappeared into the crowd, and I grabbed a beer and tried to pull myself together. My heart was beating fast, my fingers shaking. Back in the crowd I felt very alone, and I remembered how my sister had had a panic attack in Arnotts one Christmas. I wondered if I'd been spiked or if I was going crazy and then Rory was there with a girl I thought I recognised.

"Where ya been? Youse ok?"

I slugged the can, crushing it with one hand to show that everything was fine.

"You remember Jack? From school? Her mum and dad are up there on Bay View Road."

"Hey," I said, struggling to remember, confused by Kelly, my feelings.

"My Annie knows your Katie," said Jack.

Rory was raising his eyebrows, signalling to me.

"You wanna drink?" I asked.

I already knew that tonight was the night when everything changed. I'd fallen in love, grown up, become a man, drunk too much, felt happy and sad all at once, thought about my stupid Da.

"Rory?" I asked but he was shaking his head and so I took Jack to the bar and made her a vodka and orange and got myself another can.

We sat on the top step that led down to the basement and I gave Jack a cheers, my can bumping against her plastic cup.

"I don't think I knows you," I said, and I could hear I was slurring, even with the music so loud.

"Yes ya fuckin' do. Annie Walsh's sister. Brother, I guess, if that helps. You ok?"

"Jack. Yeah, I remember. I'm ok. I'm just a bit all over the place. The music. The booze. I met a girl that I liked and now she's gone. I'm sorry."

Jack put her arm around me and I rested my head on her shoulder.

"You'll be right," she said. "Big night, huh?"

She sounded calm, assured. Kelly had this fierce energy, a wild spirit, that had worked its way inside me. But Jack was different. A girl who'd grown up a boy, but from my town, someone who knew all about the detail of things and what they mean.

I wanted to tell her everything. That I felt like I was on the cusp of something. That I'd fucked up my exams and that I didn't want to be a mechanic or a butcher. That sometimes at night I'd ride out along the coast road and shut my eyes for as long as I dared. That I was happy, most of the time, that I really didn't want to die. That I wished my Da hadn't gone, even though I could barely remember him at all. That I wanted to drink tonight until I passed out. Drink so much that Kelly would step over me on the way out. That Rory would leave me slumped in a corner like Richie Reynolds and head back to Wicklow and tell my Ma I'd stayed with a friend. That I had this sense that tonight had changed me forever. That there was no going back. That I'd outgrown my small town. That I wanted to be a motorbike racer or a rock star or just someone, somewhere. Someone who was loved and loved someone back. Someone kind and calm and cool.

I wanted to tell Jack all of this, but I slumped forward, my head in her lap and she ran her fingers through my hair. I felt the baked potato in my windpipe again, hot and strange. I took her free hand in mine and squeezed her fingers and it was like she was talking to me. Telling me that she could see me, that she understood. It was like a whisper that only I could hear. 'You're a good person. You'll be ok. Life is short and you've to go with your gut and be true to yourself, who you really are'. It seemed like forever, my head in her lap, and it was like all the sadness I'd felt earlier just melted away.

It's a cliché, I know. The one night that changes your life. Like one of them dumb movies my Ma loves to watch. Young love and all that bollocks. But you know what? It's true. Me and Kelly and then me and Jack and fast forward three years and we're married and we live in New York and I realise how those hours at that party were like my version of that film. Ryan Gosling with some girl on a motorbike. And then later with my true love, someone different, but someone like me.

I'm still a kid, really. Jack too. But I'm old enough to know I ain't gonna be a rock star or a motorbike racer and that's just fine. My Ma told me that life with Jack would be difficult. That I was taking on something, someone, who's going through a huge change. But Jack's cool and the truth is so much more ordinary than my Ma might have ever expected. We go to work, we do our laundry, we watch films on TV. We've even got a cat. And I can honestly say that from that night on, the night of the party, the night I fell in love, twice, perhaps, that I've been happy, happy, happy.

Kate O'Grady

Kate O'Grady lives in Stroud. Her short stories have been long
listed/short listed or placed in Bath Flash Fiction Award, Bath
Short Story Award, Reflex Fiction Flash Fiction Competition,
The Phare Short Story Competition, Exeter Short Story
Competition, Gloucester Writers' Network Competition,
Stroud Book Festival Short Story competition, and published
in *Storgy Magazine, The Phare Literary Magazine*, and *Stroud
Short Stories Anthology*.

Becoming

At the flats, we are transforming into birds. It is happening quickly to some of us and slowly to others. Each morning, after restless sleep, we search our beds for stray feathers, running our hands over sheets and under pillows. Those of us who have already grown tails get down on all fours and peer underneath our beds for lost quills. Every day we stare into bathroom mirrors looking for further changes to our faces, our bodies, our limbs. We stroke our arms and wonder if we will mourn them when they become wings, if we will miss our feet when they become claws. We are both frightened and excited, but mostly we are excited. The truth is, we want out, we want flight, we want gone.

Vivian in Number 1 was the first to transform. She turned bald eagle in less than 24 hours. I found her wandering the downstairs hall two weeks ago, beady eyed and screeching, her razor sharp beak making frantic stabs at the wooden cubby hole unit where we keep the post, her razor sharp talons ripping the hessian carpet to shreds.

There seems to be a brief period, around twenty minutes, when speech is still available to the newly transformed, a time lag where the vestiges of human being lingers through the voice. I recognized Vivian's straight away, the shaky falsetto of the octogenarian she had so recently been, calling my name and requesting that I open a window. Only the

149

day before, I had visited her in the over heated ground floor studio she rents, and was touched then, as always, by her elegant hospitality; the delicate blue china cups, the matching plates, the ornate silver tray, the small pitcher of milk, the large slabs of fruit cake and the two white cloth serviettes folded into neat triangles.

In her flat, the day before, we had talked about the shootings, the bombings, the relentless burning of the forests, the lead slates that had fallen from the roof in the recent storms. From facing armchairs we gazed at each other and sipped our tea. I could see Vivian's nose was hardening and becoming more beak-like. Its yellow hue, its glossiness, its sharp curve at the end, were mesmerising. She glanced several times at the spread of bright orange plumage that was now visible just above my collar.

"Soon," Vivian had said as I was leaving her flat that afternoon, her index finger stroking the soft white feathers that were beginning to appear and multiply on her forehead at a rapid rate. "I think it will be soon now for me."

"Yes, soon," I replied.

The next day, on the window ledge, Vivian peered up at the pale grey February sky. A strong wind moved through her feathers and she swivelled her head to preen a few of them on her back, running her beak across the length of each. This done, she stared at me for a few seconds, and then she took off.

That wing span, that grace, that beauty.

Since then, two more of us have transformed. The Nelsons, a middle aged couple who lived in Number 5, turned sparrow and tawny owl last Thursday. We were able to pinpoint their breeds in the final hours when everything accelerates. Having pored over so many photographs in the multiple bird guides bought online during the last month, we are all experts now at identifying the birds we are becoming. Rob Nelson's stiff, flecked facial ruff, newly grown that morning, along with the large, round jet black eyes he had been staring at us with for weeks, all said owl. "You'll be a tawny," Ava from Number 4 whispered to him across my dining room table where we were all sat eating bowls of chile con carne. Alice Nelson's fawn dress perfectly matched the beige stripe of delicate feathers that extended from the corner of each eye to her hairline. Earlier in the week we had observed her, from our windows, lying face down on the garden path, twisting and turning in the dirt.

"Sparrow," we had said then to each other, mournfully nodding our heads, wistful with memories of those tiny birds we had once seen everywhere, bathing in the dust.

Kevin from Number 3 volunteered to spend the last hours of transformation with the Nelsons. Kevin was only in the early stages of bird then, just a rounding of the eyes, a slight elongation of the nose. When he emerged from the Nelsons' flat the next morning looking dazed, we all crowded around to hear the news.

"It's stunning, how quickly it all takes place at the very end," Kevin said. "The wing formation, the beaks, the shrinking, the flapping out of clothes."

We have yearned to be birds for so long, and now it is happening. We are giddy with expectation. We leave the windows wide open at all times and there is a constant chill, and the pages of our bird guides flutter in the breeze.

Kevin turned raven today. Ava and I sat at either side of him on his kitchen floor and held a hand each, letting go only when two glorious sleek black wings started to form at his shoulders. We made coffee then and watched and waited. Outside, we could hear birdsong. It was everywhere.

Now it is just the two of us, and Ava and I wander the empty flats of our neighbours, going in and out of rooms, picking up photos and objects that once belonged to them, and placing them back down. Ava's blue tail feather is visible beneath her Arran sweater, and she has snow white feathers at her throat. Our hair is turning turquoise.

At night we dream of birds, great flocks of them, moving through the sky.

Today is the first day of spring, and we are becoming kingfishers. We are blue and orange and beautiful. We sit on the couch and hold hands, and we can feel the moving and shifting and rearranging of our internal organs.

"Are you glad?" Ava asks me.

"Yes," I reply.

I lift my right arm, my arm that is already becoming wing, and Ava rests her iridescent head against my chest. Through the open window I can see a line of trees. Beyond the trees there are fields, and beyond the fields there is the river. When it is time, we will fly there.

Jyoti Patel

Jyoti Patel is a London-based author. She is a graduate of the University of East Anglia's Creative Writing Prose Fiction MA and winner of the 2021 #Merky Books New Writers' Prize. Her writing has previously been published as part of *WePresent's* 'Literally' Series. Her debut novel, *The Things That We Lost*, will be published by #Merky Books in January 2023.

Once

WHEN I SEE you again, you are standing two people in front of me in the queue to the self-checkouts at a Tesco Express in Ealing, your little finger curled around the handle of a pint of blue-topped milk. Your other hand rests on the nape of the woman standing beside you, her hair short and curly and shimmering like silk. In truth, I don't notice her until a moment later, because despite the signature black cap perched backwards on your head and the green corduroy jacket I bought you for Christmas and the irrefutable fact that it must be you simply from the shape of your stance, my mind loops back and trips over the detail of the milk; you always drank semi-skimmed with me.

Nevertheless, it is you. My mind is alight with flames, my chest pounding. You have a pint of milk and a new girlfriend and I, I have a box of tampons and a pack of extra-long matches that rattle slightly in my hand. I feel there is some shame in both, so I tuck one under each of my arms and then it suffocates me; the sheer dissonance of the fact that I would now be mortified of you seeing me with sanitary products when once, I put my index finger into your mouth after a day of pastries and coffee and beer and pizza to remove a dried little chilli flake that was bothering you, wedged between your gum and a wisdom tooth, the one by the bottom left corner of your mouth, scooping it away with my nail. Once, there was a time when you would wander into the bathroom and perch yourself against the edge of the sink whilst I was showering, just for a chat. Once, not so long ago, I could close my eyes and trace every blemish and mole on your body as though they were a constellation and you, the galaxy.

I grasp for the shadows of these things, wondering how they could have ever been true.

Here I am, trying to make sense of this new shape of you, pattern matching it against the outline of us. I think specifically back to the moment I knew you loved me. It was not when you told me but, rather, three weeks before you spoke the words; we were on a plane to Berlin and I had a migraine and you came to the bathroom with me where there was barely room for one body let alone two. You rubbed between my shoulders as I threw up in the tiny steel sink. When it started backing up you murmured gently 'oh please fuck no' whilst keeping one hand on me and with the other, with the other you reached for the plug hole and lifted it up. I watched, heaving, my eyes wide with nausea and wider still with horror. Now, just a little over a year later, I can't even bear the thought of you turning around and seeing my face without makeup, a box of tampons stuffed under my arm. I cannot fathom how you were once willing to dip your fingers into a pool of my sick and now, now I cannot even summon the will to call your name and say hello.

It's delicate, intimacy, and I think of how beautiful it is to make and how easy it is to break, like a nest woven together from spun sugar. I recall everything we once built, all we had, and how it has cooled to ash now, colourless and fragmented.

I hold all of this as I watch you, both of you, and I don't wonder how you are, or if you finally got that promotion, or if you ever did have that small hard lump the size of a blueberry looked at. Instead, I wonder if you still skip the last step when going down the stairs. If you still pinch the wicks of candles to put them out. If you still grow steadily rowdier when you drink more than a large glass of red. I wonder about these things, these things that once made you you, because if the milk has changed then what else has.

Her name is Cla(i)re, the woman beside you with the golden curls whose neck you are caressing. I wonder how it's spelt as you suggest ordering an Indian instead of preparing the Wellington you promised her tonight. She tells you she'd love that, honey. This closing word, the gooey thickness of it, seems to congeal at the very bottom of my lungs. My lips part when I hear you speak. Your voice glitters in the air, like pieces of glass that have shattered by the heat of a fire. Something in me wants to reach out and touch them, to feel those sharp jagged edges again, just for a moment.

Her neck looks soft, it's icing on a cake. The fact you can so casually grip this vulnerable part of her seems to cascade and crash in me like a riptide. The memory of you against the reality of you. The version she sees of you against the knowledge I hold of you.

She sneezes then and her curls bob and ripple and the whole thing is sweet and delicate, and although until this point I have refused to compare myself to her, something breaks in me at the sound of her endearing little sneeze, like a drop too many, bursting a dam. There is a fragility to her that I know you would adore, and I watch the hand that was resting on the nape of her neck move to a strand of her perfectly curled hair that looks so much like it came from a cocoon. I think of my coarse dark hair, which has never and could never resemble anything remotely close to silk, how it's dull and heavy without even the decency to hold a wave. You wrap a strand of her buttery hair around your finger, stroke it, then place it back as it was. It's so quick, this movement, stolen almost, and on one level I am aware I have trespassed just to witness it and on another, on another my mind is full of how you used to do this to me. I think of how the memory of my hair on your fingertips must feel shameful and small and powdery compared to the generous shining lock your fingers were curled around just a moment ago. It reminds me of how quickly and unexpectedly that delicious caress turned into an anguish I had never anticipated from you, not once.

My eyes fall again to the little finger on your other hand, the one that's functioning as a hook for the pint of milk, and I wonder how it isn't numb with cold by now. There it is, red but resolute. You step forward and I watch you, the pair of you, because together you are one, and it is as one that you move towards the till, your hand on her shoulder as you scan the blue-topped pint of milk that I still can't understand. She reaches into her pockets for coins which she feeds one by one into the machine. She has perfect change, for which you congratulate her, but of course she does, for everything about her is tidy and measured, like a carefully-wrapped present.

Your hand is again on her nape and, though your grip looks light and protective and as though it is as effortless as anything, the hairs on my arms rise up, reminding me that this was how it all started for us; just an innocent hand on the back of my neck, your fingers slowly tightening to leave dapples across my skin - purple, green, yellow - makeup barely covering them, the friends I was forbidden to see, the clothes I was shamed for wearing, the confiscation of my phone, my keys, my car, and at times, my will.

These memories sit like shadows under every one of your movements now, waiting, and I wonder if she has already noticed them below, stirring, dogging your love, as they did for me, until that night; the night I collected the scraps of myself, set them alight and escaped under cover of the thick dark fumes left curling around you.

You leave without a glance back.

As you turn the corner and I brave a step forward, my gaze follows the shape of the pair of you, the way you are with one another, and it so reminds me of the pair of us, and the asymmetrical shape we made together, once.

Rachel Sloan

Rachel Sloan is an art historian, curator and writer. Born and raised in the suburbs of Chicago, she has called the UK home for most of her adult life. Her work has appeared in *The Antigonish Review, Elsewhere, Moxy, Stonecrop Review, STORGY,* and *Canopy:* an anthology of writing for the Urban Tree Festival (2021). She was Highly Commended in the 2020 Bridport Prize, runner-up in the 2021 Urban Tree Festival writing competition, longlisted for the 2021 Nan Shepherd Prize in nature writing and a finalist in the 2021 London Independent Story Prize.

Still Life With Lemon

He never misses a thing. Not a breadcrumb, not an apple pip, not the tiniest paring of cheese. Nothing in the house escapes his notice.

I've worked for Master C for a year. I could do worse, I know: he pays me a fair wage and I've a place to sleep that isn't too cold or too mouse-ridden and I'm no more overworked than any other maid-of-all-work. And I've enough to eat, even if it's the same day in and day out: porridge, brown bread, weak beer. A salted herring once or twice a year, if I'm lucky. If it weren't for my job it would never have occurred to me to want more.

Master C is a painter. Some painters paint people or trees or houses. Not him. He paints food. Feasts laid out on silver dishes, roemers full up with gold and garnet wine. Or so I've heard. I'm not allowed into his studio. Only Cook's permitted, and grudgingly at that: someone has to prepare the dishes, after all.

Cook curses him constantly. Says she has twice as much work as in a normal household: dishes to eat, dishes to paint. *Never enough bloody time to catch my breath*, she mutters, *let alone do the shopping.* So that's my job. Buying the ingredients for painted meals. *Mind you don't let anyone at the market cheat you, girl*, she orders, counting out the

161

coins. *And don't even think of sneaking a mouthful on the way home. He'll know.* So I'm shoved out the door three times a week with a different shopping list every time.

The meat market's the worst: blood, flies, leering butcher's boys, and all for what? A hunk of beef that no one will ever see when it's minced and hidden in a pie. The fish stalls scare me: heaps of wriggling eels, crabs clacking their claws like jointed automata. But the vegetable market is a different kind of torture, baskets of cherries and redcurrants tumbled like rubies, asparagus so fresh it looks waxed, strawberries whose fragrance seeps into my dreams. The spice merchant's: golden curls of mace, nutmegs like musket balls, woody quills of cinnamon, a scent that makes me stagger, punch-drunk. I could live there, I could. But all of it disappears into my bags and baskets, and then Cook takes it and does whatever she does with it and it vanishes into Master's studio and is never seen again. And I sit on the end of a kitchen bench, spooning porridge, supping beer.

Until the day Master C's apprentice quits.

Nobody knows why he's there one day and gone the next. He didn't seem particularly unhappy. He didn't make off with anything. All we know is that Master's in a foul mood and we're walking on eggshells. Cook says he has an important commission (*from a councilman, no less*) and he's only just got started and he's not likely to find another apprentice in time. And then the next day as I'm polishing the silver he appears in the doorway. *You, girl.* (He's never bothered to learn my name.) *I've been watching you work. You're careful and quick. I like that. I have a few jobs for you. I wouldn't ordinarily, but you'll do, in a pinch.* Before I can blink I'm in his studio with a muller in my hand and a bottle of linseed oil and little heaps of red ochre and weld and lead white in front of me. And when I finally uncurl my cramped fingers and flex my aching wrists, I look up and see I'm hemmed in on all sides by feasts.

The same tabletop, over and over again, framed in black, laid with a crumpled white cloth, all that varies is the silver and glass and the food. A platter of oysters like scattered coins, a snow-white bread roll broken in two, a roemer of white wine. An overflowing dish of grapes and peaches and apples you could reach into the canvas and pluck out. A salmon steak rosy in its crisped skin, studded with capers, a bowl of olives wet and shiny as eyes. A whole lobster, a stalk-eyed scarlet monster. In every one a lemon balances, half-naked, on the table's edge, the pebbled peel falling away in a spiral, the pith the colour of goose-down, the flesh shining like sunlit ice.

My mouth waters. My stomach's pinched, it's hours since my last dose of porridge, bread and beer. My head spins, such mad abundance and none of it is real. *None of it.* And then I see the real thing laid out on a table before Master's easel. A blue-and-white bowl of olives, another of strawberries. Walnuts and hazelnuts cracked and whole, scattered shards of nutshell. The lemon lolling in its half-undone skin. And in the middle a huge pie, its crust sanded with sugar, broken open, spilling spiced mincemeat like a heap of jewels and suddenly I can't breathe. That pie costs months of my wages. I know because I bought every ingredient with money that wasn't mine. Cook must have sweated over it for the better part of a day. And all for some rich man to just look at it. He'll never be able to smell the spices, feel the crust crumble under his tongue, taste the richness of the mincemeat, curl up in the warmth of a full belly. (But no, surely he will. A man who can waste his money on a painting of food has to have enough left in his pockets for the real thing.)

Master, I say.

He looks annoyed. No one expects a maid to speak. *Yes?*

And I want to ask him *how can you do this? Don't you understand this is strange, disgusting, wrong?* but what comes out is *the lemon. Why do you put one in every painting?*

He snorts. *See this?* Oh God, he's picked it up, is holding it inches from my nose. I've never seen one in the flesh before. I don't buy the lemons from the market. They arrive in wooden boxes from the orangery in The Hague, swaddled like babies. They're spirited into his studio before anyone can unwrap them. All that sunny yellow and translucent white too close to my eyes, my mouth. I want to lean forward and bite into it. *D'you have any idea how difficult it is to render all those textures, the skin, the pith, the flesh, in paint? It's a way of showing my skill without crowing too loud about it. Nothing more.* He puts it back. *All that talk isn't getting my greens and whites mixed.*

Next day is Sunday and I'm still thinking about those paintings while I shiver beside Cook in the servants' corner of the pews. The sermon is one of the pastor's favourites: *vanity of vanities, all is vanity* and I look around and see the rich folk looking pious across the aisle and I think I understand. I'd bet a month's wages that several of them own one of Master's painted feasts. I'd bet another month's wages that they sat down to a banquet yesterday, and didn't eat too badly the other days either. They know food and drink should only be for holding body and soul together and they're not meant to enjoy it – Pastor beats it into them every Sunday – but they know they'll keep indulging no matter what. Looking at a painting while they stuff themselves, a painting that reminds them how rich and powerful, how sinful and foolish they are, is another way of doing penance. A penance that lets them enjoy the feel of their souls twisting on the rack.

How utterly stupid.

If I could afford oysters and strawberries, pies and sweetmeats and wine, I wouldn't lash myself over it. I wouldn't hide them and throw away the key and pretend that made me virtuous. I'd sink my teeth in. I wouldn't leave a scrap.

After this the answer's obvious: steal.

It's almost too easy, and yet it's not. Master C keeps me on in his studio. Now, along with mixing paints, I carry in the dishes from the kitchen, though he doesn't trust me to arrange them. So when he starts on a small painting of a dish of oysters, I make sure to hide a spare, unshucked, in my pocket to replace the one I'll take. I wait until he's gone out in search of a candle and then I do the swap. My heart's knocking so hard against my ribs I'm sure he'll hear it when he returns, but nothing happens. I wait until dark to slip downstairs to the yard and prise it open with a borrowed knife. It looks so beautiful in the moonlight, like a giant tarnished guilder, but then I tip it into my mouth and *UGH* it's disgusting, like swallowing a mouthful of snot and seawater and I want to spit it out but I don't. I hide the shell in my pocket but lie awake rigid and dry-mouthed, remembering Cook's warning. First thing the next morning I sneak down to the canal and dump it.

It should put me off, but it doesn't. The next theft: a single hazelnut, its shell the colour of a squirrel's coat. I curl my finger round it like a marble and hook it out of the pile before I bring it into the studio, crack it open between two stones in the yard. It crumbles between my teeth like butter and earth and I'm shivering with happiness. I don't even wish I had another, it was enough. I sweep up all the bits of shell and they follow the oyster into the canal, but every time I pass that corner of the yard I think I see a chip lying between the cobbles and I start to sweat, even though a second glance just shows bare stone.

The strawberry is child's play. I don't even bother replacing it like for like, I twist up a scrap of red cloth and push it into the bowl and rearrange the others on top of it and you'd never guess it was missing. I'm terrified it'll get squashed in my pocket but by the time I take it out it doesn't even have a bruise. It smells like summer and tastes like roses and this time I don't have to worry about hiding the evidence: I eat the leaves.

And so it goes: a blackcurrant, a redcurrant, a fingerful each of salt and pepper dabbed up from a paper twist. A caper, a grape, a half-mouthful of wine, a shard of piecrust the size of my little fingernail. I'm beginning to think I'll get away with it when I'm drying a platter in the scullery after supper and Cook comes up behind me and says *Master seems to think there're mice in his studio* and I flinch before I can stop myself. *I told him I'd keep an eye out.* She pulls a little bag of stuivers from her pocket and says *I think this is what you're owed for this month. Best you be careful, girl.* I don't know why she put her neck on the line for me but I'm not fool enough to question it.

Before first light I'm on the road to Amsterdam with a bundle on my back. If I hurry I can make it before nightfall. I can disappear there. I'm sure I'll find work, a maid's always needed. But let my new employer be a brewer, merchant, lawyer, doctor – I've had enough of painters.

In one pocket I carry my wages and the heel of a loaf. In the other is a lemon. Every few minutes I slip my fingers in to cradle it, to feel the pitted smoothness of its skin, to breathe in the sharp sunny scent that rubs off on my skin. When the sun's high in the sky I sit down on the grass, finish the bread in a few gulps and take out the lemon. One more sniff and I bite in.

It's harder and more slippery than an apple and I think the rind will never break but when it does my tongue shrivels and my teeth judder and the insides of my cheeks nearly explode and juice splashes down my chin and I feel like I've been cudgelled between the eyes and

Oh it is sour

Oh it is bitter

But I make myself keep eating and finally, finally

It is sweet.

Kailash Srinivasan

Kailash Srinivasan is an Indian-Canadian author living in Vancouver. His narratives often highlight fractures of different kinds: personal, societal, economic, religious, and political. He also writes about class, injustice and inequality. His prose and poetry have appeared in several Canadian and international literary journals, including *Handwritten & Co., Midway Journal, Snarl, Hunger, Coachella Review, Selkie, Antilang, Lunch Ticket* and others. His short story, *Bikhari*, was the runner-up in the 2022 *Prime Number Magazine* Awards for Poetry & Short Fiction. His work has also been shortlisted for *Into the Void* Fiction Prize and longlisted for the Bath Short Story Award. He has an MFA in Creative Writing from UBC and is working on his first novel.

Coconut

very evening at 7, the brahmin priest at the Ganesha temple cracks freshly washed coconuts on the cement stairs outside to offer to the Lord. He's inside the sanctum, moving the oil lamp in circles with one hand, ringing the handbell with the other. Keerthi, my sister, giggles at his jiggling belly and breasts. Devotees stand in separate lines: men left, women right; no funny-funny at the temple.

Keerthi and I flank the stairs. It's difficult to predict the trajectory of the coconut after it slaps the ground. There's competition as usual: boys poised hawk-like. Somu, our next-hut neighbour, grins. I grow, snapping my fingers to get Keerthi's attention.

"If Somu pulls your hair, kick him in the nuts."

"OK, Anjali Akka."

I'm the elder sister at twelve. She's still a baby at eight, with so much to learn. *Grow up faster,* I tell her sometimes.

The priest is at the topmost stair, grabbing two at a time from the pile beside him. When the coconuts make contact, they snap into dozens of pieces. In seconds, they're gone. I clinch a big slice while Keerthi is empty-handed. Somu's brimming – hands full, two between his teeth, two in the top pocket. I wish for him to get constipated and never be able to shit again. We go behind the temple and run the tap to wash off the turmeric. I snap mine in half, one for me, one for her.

Dinner is leftovers Laxmi auntie gave Amma at work. Ma cleans her house and a few others every day. Her bones creak at night.

"Didi is nice," Ma says, "but the husband *stares*."

Appa's teeth gnash. Ma says, "Don't worry, I'm careful. He tries anything I'll crack a brick on his face."

Appa doesn't want her to work, but there aren't many jobs around, and we need money. Appa thinks when the bottle-making factory finally opens, everyone will have jobs. Five years have passed since the minister announced it as his election promise.

We get a piece of fish each. "Shanti, remind me to pay school fees," Appa says. Worry lines claw his forehead. Brick-laying work is hard and seasonal. Sometimes there's demand. Sometimes Appa waits and waits for a truck that isn't coming.

"Watch for fish bones," Amma says. Keerthi and I giggle as Appa's eyes widen. Amma is a repeat offender: she moves to other subjects even before others have finished talking.

The fish is hot. Milk would've helped, but we aren't allowed to drink any. We sell milk from our two goats to the nearby dairy.

***

Somu is on his grandma's lap. He's almost a whale at fourteen and still in grade eight. She's feeding and singing to him in a shaky voice, "Sweet, lovely child, eat-eat-eat, grow-grow-grow."

I giggle at the idea of him growing more and she glowers.

"Shoo, born to a cursed mother."

"Ma's not cursed. Somu is. He got a zero in the maths test. Tell you how much I got?"

"Any good? You'll only ever be a maid, like your mother."

I pick up a stone and let it fly. It crashes into her knee, and Keerthi and I take off to school.

At noon, we wait for Amma. The only set of keys is with her. Keerthi groans. I'm hungry too. I go behind the house where our goats are tied while Keerthi keeps a watch. If the dairy gets less milk this one time, no one will die. At least it will keep us full until Ma returns. But there's no *maaah* at my approach like there is every day.

"Keerthi," I yell, running back, kohl leaking from my eyes. They are missing.

We rush in opposite directions, checking everywhere – temple, pond, fields – and find nothing.

Amma wails when she hears. "Aiyo-aiyo. The thief will vomit blood, his intestines will explode." An hour later, Appa returns, and when he learns, rushes to the back to check for himself, as though I may have imagined it.

"Found them?" Amma asks when Appa returns goatless.

"Yes, allow me to take them out of my pocket." Then, realizing he's being short with her, shakes his head.

The following day, Somu's grandmother says, "Must be in someone's biryani by now," her mouth red from the paan.

***

It's late evening, and no sign of Appa. Amma mumbles: "Please protect my husband, Ganesha." As the hours pass, she gets restless, praying to Ganesha, running out to check, then in, out again. Keerthi clucks her tongue.

"Whack you. You'll only know what I feel after you get married."

"Yuck."

Just then, two men enter with a stretcher made of bamboo and gunny sacks. Appa is on it, arms and legs bandaged, pain pinching his bruised face. He winces, and Ma begins: "Aiyo-aiyo, Rama, Krishna, Govinda," invoking all the deities she knows.

Finally, Appa says, "Shanti, stop. Your shouting hurts more."

They found Appa next to a ditch after the men he accused of stealing the goats beat him with hockey sticks.

"Aiyo-aiyo, maggots will fill their mouths," Ma curses.

After dinner, the four of us spread out on thin straw mats. Soon, I hear Appa groan: "If only these girls had a brother, all our worries – ," he trails off.

If we had a brother, Appa would've sent him to the site in his place, and we wouldn't have lost a day's pay.

***

"Six months' rest minimum," the curt doctor informs, "depending on how the legs heal." He points at Appa's x-rays, expecting us to follow.

Ma returns from the pharmacy, and Appa says, "What will we eat if we keep spending our money on medicines?" He glances at the two of us, and his shoulders deflate. Amma stops going to work because Appa needs help with everything, even going to the toilet, four times a day. Her Madams find new maids within days.

For dinner, it's thin, bland rice gruel again.

***

My teacher calls out the names of students whose fee is overdue in front of the entire class.

Somu smirks.

"What are *you* laughing at, dumbass?» I shout.

"Watch your mouth," says the teacher.

The house is still and dark in the afternoon, except for the light from the mud stove, the moist wood crackling. Amma's using a hand-fan to kick up the fire. Dirty dishes and clothes pile in a corner.

My tumbler has more gruel than usual.

"What's wrong?" I ask. She shudders at that.

"Did a crow pluck your tongues?" Keerthi asks.

"Don't think we love you less," Amma says to me.

Appa's hand tremors before he says, "Jili, there's no money to send you to school."

"No more gruel to torture our mouths either, please." Keerthi chuckles.

"We can't... sorry."

Ma keeps stirring the pot, even though the bottom burns.

I pretend like I didn't hear. "Have math exam tomorrow, then chemistry, then geography, oof."

"They're a nice family, big house in the city. You'll be... happy."

I cry, I beg, but they stay silent. Keerthi sobs into my neck.

Nothing more than a maid.

***

The engine coughs. Appa hops to the queue, crutches rattling, two flimsy bus tickets in hand. I want Amma to say,

She's not going anywhere.
No daughter of mine will wash dirty dishes of others.
We'll manage.

But she stands there, fists clenched by her sides, a melancholic expression on her face, like trying to remember something forgotten. Keerthi rips my skirt, trying to keep me from leaving. Even when Amma wrests her away, she breaks free and runs after the bus screaming, "Appa, take me, take me. Akka loves school." A large cloud of dust swallows her.

***

My Madam wears loose pants, a striped shirt, her hair long and curly. Her daughter, Ria, clutches her legs, looking at me shyly. There's a scent in the air. Rose? Marble floors, AC on full blast. The rooms are so far apart, I'll need a bicycle to go from one to the other. Madam shows me to my room. It has a cot, a mattress, almirah and a dresser.

Appa's afraid to sit on their pastel sofa. "No-no," he says when she insists, thinking he may dirty it.

"Was the bus ride pleasant?" Madam asks. "You must be starving."

"Nothing for me," Appa says with folded hands. "I'll leave now." He gets to his feet, steadies his crutches.

My heart jumps, a rock in my throat.

"Be good," he says, angling away, not meeting my eyes. My stomach sinks.

***

My room is bigger than three huts side-by-side. Madam gives me a toothbrush, hair comb, a soap that smells, I imagine, like Ganesha must. Sleeping on a nice mattress should put me to sleep, but I can't sleep, not until my eyes prickle from being open for too long. Three days since Appa left. I'm angry at him for being poor, for taking away the chance owed to me. Even with the air-conditioner on, my body blazes. I drift off to memories of myself in the first row, my hand going higher and higher, hoping to be picked to answer the teacher's question.

The rice cooker jolts me out of sleep in the morning. It hisses *Wake up, waake upp, waaaake uppp.*

There's a rap on the door.

"It's seven. Hope the sound didn't bother you," Madam says in a politely biting tone.

"Sorry, Madam, won't happen again." My face is hot and ashamed.

A monkey dancing to its master's beats: *Yes Madam, no Madam, okay Madam.*

She must've noticed. Honey colours her words. "How many times to tell you? Not to call me *Madam*. Say *Auntie*."

I wash their clothes, their dishes, mop the slippery floors with a dirty rag, scrub the toilet bowl till the ceramic twinkles, scrape the grout between tiles till my fingers twinge. Every morning I watch Ria go to school in her uniform.

Madam's friends have no hobbies. They get together every day to complain about things. One of them asks me, "Do you have a sister? Does she know housework?"

I pray for hours that night.

***

I'm allowed one call every two weeks. Those mornings I'm up before the first light. First, I call the village grocer – the only one with a phone – and beg him to inform my parents. He always grumbles, slamming his phone down. If I receive a missed call, it means someone is at the shop. I ring back to either hear Amma's hurried breath, the gulp in Appa's voice or Keerthi's cackle and wait for my next call even as she tells me she's saving up all her stories to tell them to me when we meet.

"Thank you for feeding this family," Amma says.

I don't tell her I start at five and work until nine p.m. Even Sundays. Then I go to sleep and start again. That my only friend here is the radio madam has given me.

She asks me if I've eaten.

I want to tell her about the beggar lady outside the temple. Every time she sees me, she says, "Don't be upset, sweetheart." People call her mad.

But I can't. Madam is nearby and always listening.

***

Madam tips a spoonful of sugar in my mouth one morning. "Happy anniversary," she chirps. "Keep the spoon. Now you have two."

On the bottom almirah shelf in my room is where I keep my separate plate, spoon, and tumbler.

She told me early on to not mix my utensils with the ones in the kitchen.

I ready Ria for school, iron her uniform.

"What's this, Dummy? Why is there still a crease on my skirt?" Ria asks, parroting her mother.

Madam and Sir chuckle at the way Ria's nose trembles when she's mad. Her bus arrives at 6 am sharp. The driver gives two honks two minutes apart. If you're not there, he won't stop even when he sees you yanking the child after you.

I pack her bag carefully, or else I'll hear, "English is *after* the maths period. Why can you never get the order right?"

***

In the movie Madam lets me watch, the heroine finally tears off her burqa to reveal the face and voice behind the country's biggest singing sensation. I'm so into it, two litres of organic milk boils and spills over the stove, the counter, leaks into the cupboard underneath.

Madam burns the skin on my elbow with hot tongs.

"Why are you so careless? You think I like doing this?" she says, handing me a tube of Boroline for the wound.

***

I scramble to help Madam when I see her wrestling with two bags, both fat with coconuts.

"It's Sir's birthday tomorrow, so I'm making coconut barfi, his favourite. Will you help?"

I strip the fruit's coarse hair; she drops two Stevia tablets in her black coffee. I run my fingers over their prickly bald heads, looking for weak areas to target; she turns on the television. I crack the hard shells open and pour the water into a tall glass. It makes my mouth water.

"Start grating," she says, neck craned, ears alert to the dialogue on the screen.

Soft coconut flesh crumbles against the clawed circular blade, falling on the steel plate below, along with darker flecks from scraping too close to the shell.

Why waste?

My arms thrum from overwork.

"Don't mix the brown bits," she thunders suddenly, and the blade almost stabs my hand. My fingertips are moist, oily from handling the shredded coconut. I can't control any longer. I want it in my mouth.

Amma's words warn me: *Don't ask. Only take things Madam gives on her own. When you ask, people think you're shameless.*

But better to ask than to steal?

"Can I have some, Madam?"

She hesitates, turns her head slowly. "This is for Sir."

I look back down.

"Add sugar and milk." She reads the recipe off her phone during an ad break she mutes.

When Sir returns in the evening, she coos, "I made these for you with my own hands, Baby," and stuffs two in his mouth.

"Want some?" Sir asks me when he catches me looking, voice gentle.

"I already ate," I stammer and, dropping my eyes, get back to work.

Later that night, I hear Madam on the phone with a friend. "Of course, you can borrow my maid for a day." She says, "Why would she mind?" and I choke back tears and continue wiping the kitchen counter.

Henry Stennett

Henry Stennett is a Brit(ish)-Jamaican writer who lives in
Bristol. During his PhD, he tried to discover antibiotics from
deep-sea sponges. While he failed in that goal, he did get to
name some new species of bacteria. After a cruel misadventure
in medical advertising, Henry is now enjoying his work as a
science communicator. He translates jargon into plain English
and shapes it into stories. *Elision* was the first short story he
wrote – he's cooking up some more.

Elision

The kind of silence you only find on early a.m. buses. The sky beyond my window is difficult to name: the wind recolours it on a whim. We used to have a name for everything, but then the names were taken away.

My task this morning is naming. We found a new fungus, glimmering white in what little light escaped the canopy. I don't have to close my eyes to be there again. The motorboat lists to the riverbank where brown (quick) greets brown (still). The river heaves its burden onto the bank; the bank sighs into silt. My skin whispers to me, stories of closeness and movement, the sheen of sweat having given it voice.

I miss humidity on mornings like these when the wind sneers through the single glazing. I pull my sleeves over my fingertips. Sometimes, I wonder at this place, only halfway my home; I imagine my lives had ____ stayed in ____ and ____ found ____ way out there instead. I don't know that ____ suits my constitution. A land the sun forgot, where figs wither on the branch. I rub my ankle where the stingy air has left me ____.

JUNGLE: THEN.

The boat rises from the water as ____ hefts our bags ashore. Beyond

181

the berth is another world of red earth and trees tilting at the sun into sweet nowhere. Petrol smell cedes to peat, decomposition, and a sour musk that must be the sweat of everything. The air is thick with life. We shoulder our packs and follow _____ to the camp, a gasp of space between the trees. There are huts on stilts and walkways between them for when the rain comes and the river stretches its limbs. _____ catches the clean wonder in my eyes and, laughing, asks if it's my first time in the jungle.

It's already dark by the time we've rearranged our things, so I'm grateful for _____ torchlight. We've decided to wash before dinner, but we won't stay clean or dry for more than a few minutes this week. _____ rests _____ hand on my forearm and clutches me for ballast every few steps. _____ tried to talk _____ out of coming a week before the flight, but _____ doesn't recognise _____ in words like _____. _____ wasn't missing this for the world.

The walkway's boards mushroom into decking, barrels brimming with rainwater, and four cubicles. I push a pail that would prefer to float beneath the green-brown gloss and pull up a thing that longs to sink. The decking groans as I waddle to the furthest cubicle; inside, I strip and pour cold water over myself. I persuade a thin lather from my bar of soap and work it around my skin. At home, I can't abide cold showers: I shriek and kvetch at my _____ in my towel and shower cap until _____ sorts the boiler out. All that time in the lab and you can't work out a simple mechanism, _____ likes to say. But this isn't home. I lift the bucket over my head to rinse myself off and lurch back to the bus with a hypnic jerk.

BUS: NOW.

Rain hurls itself against the window. Along with it, a gloom is settling in: it limps up and down the aisle, unable to choose a seat, before squeezing in next to everyone. The streetlights, headlamps, and brake lights are streaked and haloed on the glass. I unfasten my backpack and extract my notepad. Uncap my pen. Two hours until I arrive at the conference to explain what we unleashed from the jungle. Two hours to name the fungus that Unnamed us ...

Why do we name? Because we fear ambiguity. This is why _____ _____ people used to ask where I'm from – *no, really, originally.* A name tells us what to expect from someone. It describes a perimeter, delimits their possibilities. Why observe once you have a name? The hard work has been done for you: _____ _____ are angry, no one is born _____, _____ are good with money, _____ _____ excel at maths, _____ _____ can't jump, _____ are _____ or _____, _____ be crazy, _____ don't cry.

It seemed possible that the Unnaming would free us. At first, we panicked as home by home, country by country, we lost the ability to communicate certain words. But we learned to carry our terror in our stomachs like so much chewed hair. We came to understand that our collective names remained: it was the identities and identifiers that had deserted us. All of our differences flattened overnight. Without the means of describing them, would they still matter? Was prejudice possible without the names? Would the old structures evaporate? Were we finally, equivocally, equal?

JUNGLE: THEN.

"Guess on!" chuckles _____.

_____ debating _____ on a finer point of mycology. We haven't stopped working since we returned to camp. Heat and humidity aren't on our side: tissues and molecules are unravelling with every moment. I'm trying to work out how our fungus controls its host. Which cocktail of molecules would make a rat ignore its instincts like that? Psychedelics, deliriants, tremorgenics – what could they do to a mind? To clear mine, I cross the room and join my ____. The wicked tang of formaldehyde wrinkles my nose. ____ is dissecting the rat; ____ is peering under ____ elbow.

"Well, ____ lookin' rough as rats, isn't ____? Almost feel bad for the poor thing, you fossickin' through ____ guts!" ____ only receives a grunt in reply and turns to me. "Alright then are we, ____? Wanna see somethin'?" ____ leads me to ____ bench. Selects a piece of fungus, whittles, arranges, applies stains and salts, in movements slow, sudden, but always absolutely controlled. ____. There's a feeling of soothing to be found in watching a ____ perform ____ craft: it reminds me of ____ cutting glass, the brisk rasp of ____ tool as ____ swept it from edge to edge in an unerring line, the crack as ____ snapped the pane apart. How can someone be so secure in their ability? ____ drops a coverslip over ____ sample and a dark liquid blooms beneath. ____ manoeuvres the slide within the microscope's beam, stroking the focusing wheels with ____ fingertips and the deft knowing of a ____. ____ gaze is trained through the eyepiece on something beyond my ken. Sighing through ____ nostrils and working ____ jaw, ____ motions for me to approach and then cedes the eyepiece to me.

"Now, ____, say what you see."

I see hundreds of ghostly eels holding themselves erect in massed ranks; they are blue and translucent except at their tips, which are smudged darkly. And each has spit up a string of rusty peas, each a pregnant pause in possibility's course, never to be unfixed from the moment at which it met the glass.

"Are those... spores? The reddy-brown things? Coming out of those ..."

"Right on, right on! Eight ansum spores to an ascus. When one decides it's time: pop! pop! pop! off they all go, like champagne corks. Spreadin' a fine mist of spores, far as the wind'll carry 'em. On a quiet day in the woods, you can hear 'em too – a tiny hiss like a whisper. It's many a ____ that's dreamed of what they're sayin' ..."

Millions of spores loosed each day from a single mushroom. Picture them all, suffusing the air like moisture or heat, saturating your lungs; they cannot be denied; they spread, settle, and conquer. Uncountable multitudes. Every spore a promise of growth, conversion, and succession. Every spore the seed of a question that carries its own answer: how to survive, how to adapt, how to outcompete. How to establish outposts, subjugate those it encounters, or form uneasy treaties, or devastate entire kingdoms. Every word of these answers is coded in chemicals, in changes subtle and crude, genes elided, stuttered, stolen, slurred. Most of the answers will go unheard: the spores will never wake up. Many will be familiar ones. But every once in a while, with enough time or luck – which are really the same thing – there issues an answer as striking as the peal of a bell.

BUS: NOW.

Three discordant notes ring from the tannoy, followed by a crackle and the ____ voice. ____ repeats the name of a stop that isn't mine and swings ____ vessel to the side of the road.

I can't get out from under taxonomy. The logic of zoology that was extended to people as the ____ encountered and subjugated them. Observable characteristics that are supposed to reflect natural relationships. Hierarchies based on the superficial, the colours, shapes, and sizes of things. Conquest through division. ____ stolen from ____ for ____ of a different hue. Whole arbitrary bureaucracies: halves, quarters, eighths, and sixteenths. Drops, even. Purity and superiority. The stigmas survive to this day; we think in the same organising terminology of bloodlines and breeding.

To be ____ like me is to be nowhere and everywhere at once. Excluded from both for belonging to the other. ____ for the purposes of jokes, but not when it comes to reacting to them. Definitely not ____ to ____ ____ in the street, when the pawing words of their catcalls turn to threats and slurs; nor to the ____ ordering me to stand against the airport wall. But not ____, and overreacting, when I tell these stories. To most people I know, I'm not ____ and not ____ depending on the circumstances, whenever it suits them.

I'd hoped that the Unnaming would free me, but it was a foolish hope. We can still comprehend the differences that we have been taught to recognise in each other, we simply cannot find the words to communicate them. The old lie (what has ____ got to do with it? I don't see ____!) still lives, only now nobody can speak it. Our only route out has been walled off. How can we resolve what we cannot name?

My mind is tired, my body stiff from hours in an unyielding seat. I rearrange my hips and shoulders and rest my eyes.

JUNGLE: THEN.

I come to at five as the first rosy fingers of light unfurl into our world. Parting the petals of the mosquito net, I creep into the morning, flip and flop to the doorway, stretch my arms to tap its brow. ____, smoking across the way, extends a hand in greeting, and I wave back. The ____ all seem to know my name – they grin and call to me when we pass on the planks – I suppose it's a relief to host a _____ who isn't _____. I've noticed this whenever I've travelled to places where the people are _____: the _____ take an immediate shine to me. I'm unusual to them, but they don't treat this difference with distrust. On the flight here a _____ _____, _____, in _____ _____, cast glances my way once I'd settled in _____ row, and sprang from _____ seat as soon as we were cruising. _____ was in such a hurry that _____ left _____ phone behind, so after a while, I walked it up the plane to _____. _____ smiled at me then and muttered _____ thanks when I helped _____ to retrieve _____ bag from the overhead compartment. Did _____ learn anything? Or simply decide I was one of the good ones?

Breakfast is already waiting in the mess hall. I flip through a book left open on the table and slip into a world of pencil and watercolours: tail rackets, blue throats, and wings crisp with wind. _____ hand, waving in front of my face, brings me back; _____ cheeks are stuffed with noodles and glee. _____ has arrived too: _____ peels _____ cigarette from _____ bottom lip and eases into a chair.

"_____, how is it going with you this nice morning?" Heaping _____ into a mug. "Pass me, please, the water cooker?" Motioning to the kettle at my elbow. "I love this chocolate drink! It gives me such a... kick! I think we will be needing our energy today. Are you prepared already for the expedition?"

I nod. Today's the day. We're setting off early for a spot _____ knows, where the giant rats gather. Where we hope to find our fungus.

"What a pretty place! I am so glad to be in the forest, with all of the trees around. And so many creatures! Did you hear the sounds tonight? Awesome! For sure, awesome."

_____ starts to name some of the members of that raucous chorus: the waves of insect stridulation, shimmery plinks of birdsong, whooping frogs and primates. ____ interrupts.

"Love for nature is in my blood. We ____ have explored for a long time; we learned sailing and mapmaking from the ____ and then we won their colonies. Including this country. For two hundred years we kept it – still, some of our churches are here! Without us, there is no civilisation here, no roads, schools, or technology. And how do your people thank us, ____?" I can only see ____ peripherally, so I can't gauge ____ expression, but ____ lifts the bill of ____ baseball cap out of ____ eyes. "Do you know their name for the proboscis monkey here? It translates to ____. Ha! You are seeing the resemblance?"

____ pushes ____ ____ hair off ____ forehead, presents ____ profile, and closes ____ eyes for a beat – suddenly they and ____ mouth flash open as ____ produces a strangled hee-haw that bounces off the ceiling. I hide behind my coffee while ____ gathers ____ things and regains ____ feet.

"That's not a bad impression, ____! And, yes, thank ____ for the ____, for bringing their technology so that our mountains are covered in concrete instead of wood, and for taking so much away with them ... Something you may not know about the proboscis monkey: it is a proud creature, and it will starve itself to death in a zoo. Like my people, it will not be kept. If we're lucky we will see some on the river today. I'll see you at the boat."

____ whistles as ____ strolls away, twirling ____ cup from a finger. I'm loath to turn my gaze back to the table, where ____ has already fixed ____ eyes on my face.

"I think you are a rational person, ____, so you will agree with me. Many people now are oversensitive. They are emoting before they think – they are ruled by their hearts, you would say? Today, for sure, it is not possible to express an opinion. You cannot have a reasonable, rational debate. They shut you down; they call you these crazy names! You are a ____, or a ____ ____, for disagreeing with how they are rewriting history. They are twisting historical facts to fit their modern politics. To these people, the great ____ ____ are now ____. They talk about genocide and theft where, in reality, these ____ brought enlightenment everywhere they went. Can you explain to me, where would this island be today without your country and my own? For sure, nothing but famine and disease. Even now, they don't appreciate the riches of this land. They burn down the jungle while we hurry to record and protect the biodiversities."

It's like the hundredth time someone touches your ____ and, once again, you allow the moment to pass unremarked. Because you don't want to make a scene, you have to work with this person. Or the words simply won't come.

"But we are ____, ____, we are since school being trained to think rationally. This is the only way to discourse if we are to achieve things. We know this. The evidence is all around us. Rational thinking has given us GPS so that even here your mobile can tell you exactly where you are. It has given us a generator powering the lights and kitchen, even all the way out here. Electricity in a jungle, ____! It is a technological miracle. And, today, we will use the same rational scientific method to study this super cool fungus and solve the problem of how it is for the first time infecting a mammal."

A universe stuck in your throat.

"The great mystery is this process of the host jump. Most pathogens are only very recently infecting us. They waited in the sea and soil, apparently harmless, for a ____ person, for a foothold. That first encounter, ____, when the host and the invader of it are totally unprepared for one another – wow! I mean, what happens? It must be like when the first ship landed in the ____ ____. Two cultures, two languages, two ways of being are thrown together. What will be emerging? Can you imagine?"

Yes, I can imagine: the rasp of the hull on the unspoiled sand, the perfection of the intervening silence, held, held, and broken by boots crashing through the clear seawater lapping at caulk and tar, and soon by gunfire, and screams.

"Most often, the pathogen is failing to establish an infection. But, after a short time – only decades or centuries – the pathogen adapts. So intense are the selection pressures that it jumps the species barrier. Evolution happens in the one sudden leap! There is a wonderful paper published recently, about the *Cordyceps* fungus. One species has learned to attack truffles because the insects that it usually infects live close by. That is a jump across the Kingdoms of life, ____! Animal to fungus! It is unprecedented. All it required was proximity and time. So I do not think this jump to rats should surprise us. And from rat... who knows?"

To the river, to the boat, upstream, farther back into time, to the primaeval world of untouched forest. We putter to shore and a small clearing in the trees. ____ hammers home a mooring pin and ties up. Despite the heat, we button our sleeves and tuck our trousers into our socks. ____ hands out the bottles and we drench ourselves in DEET. Mephitic clouds catch at the back of my throat. ____ sprays ____ palms and rubs them over ____ face, squeezing ____ eyes tight against the chemical sting. ____ stops me with a hand on my shoulder before I can do the same: "You won't need that here, it's not like the camp. This is primary forest: very few mosquitoes. But fire ants we still need to worry about. Everyone! Rubber boots on, and then we go! We won't want to be walking uphill in the full heat of the day!"

____ leads the way into the bush, and ____ takes the rear. Both produce machetes and ＿＿ hacks at the undergrowth periodically, as if bored. I'm in awe, callow as an ＿＿; I don't know where to look, so I try to see everything at once. The green soaks greenery in a greener green. ＿＿ and ＿＿ have developed a more efficient way of seeing: they understand what constitutes a threat, looking through what distracts us to the crucial. Sometimes, one of our ＿＿ hushes us and we freeze, thighs rat trap taught. The minutes flow like molasses. Finally, ＿＿ and ＿＿ exchange glances, and we continue.

Up the slope. Forty minutes to gain one hundred metres. One by one, we materialise on the plateau with shuddering lungs. The air has changed: wisps of mist wend between the trees and wind themselves around the green, ushered by the breeze. From our newfound vantage, we can see into the valley, to a wink of the coruscating river and across to the rising hills. ＿＿ calls us over, but it takes a few moments to distinguish ＿＿ from the visual din. We gather around the spot ＿＿ indicates while ＿＿ searches our faces for any sign of recognition. Shrugs and laughs all around.

"But, ＿＿, this is your speciality! No? Well, then. Look, how the earth has been dragged away, where these leaves are piled up. An animal has hidden something here..." ＿＿ inserts the toecap of ＿＿ boot and carefully lifts it to reveal a hollow the size of a shoebox.

"A rat burrow!" – a jolt of recognition from ＿＿, who launches into a monologue about scatter-hoarding and behavioural trade-offs. ＿＿, sitting on ＿＿ haunches, rifles through the larder's contents, shaking ＿＿ head and muttering. ＿＿ summons ＿＿ and the pair speak urgently in ＿＿.

"What have you got there, ＿＿?" I venture. The air has the sweet-sharp scent of a storm rolling in: ozone born of lightning's first flickers.

＿＿ straightens up and tosses something my way: a fruit the size and colour of a lit coal. It gleams in my palm, dense, and oozing where its skin has been abraded.

"Do you know what this is, ____? Oil palm fruit. They slash and burn the forest to grow it. But, this region is protected: there shouldn't be oil palm for twenty kilometres. The rats can't travel that far. And, yet, here we have oil palm fruit. We have to report this, it could mean illegal logging, plantations..."

____ has taken a broken fruit from the burrow and is interrogating the orange flesh with a pencil. ____ spools white wool around ____ tool and, catching my eye, mouths: "Fungus".

A boom of thunder swallows ____ bawls; the echoes skitter like skipped stones before dissolving in the rain. Water cannons from above. It's inescapable, it makes rivers and cascades of the ground as we slog after ____ and ____. All I can do is stare at my shoes, and hold the hand behind me and the hand in front. The rain flogs my back and streams from my forehead.

Suddenly, the stinging stops. We've found shelter amongst the buttress roots of a monstrous tree. Overhead, its leaves shake, sifting the deluge into a soft volley. Beyond our magic circle, the rain still falls in ropes. ____ is with us again; ____ must have led us to ____. ____ pushes ____ hair out of ____ eyes and yells words lost to the incredible crashing. ____ grabs ____ by the shoulder and swivels ____ to face where ____ pointing. At the same instant, we all see it: a heap of fiery fruit, and, clinging to the summit, a rat, about a foot long. Its eyes are gently closed. It could be sleeping, but for the pale stalk erupting from the nape of its neck. Impossibly slender, the stalk gropes its way skyward and blooms into hundreds of filigree grooves and protrusions that describe something like a large white walnut. The mushroom sways slightly in the wind. In the shifting light, thrown into relief against the spray, a strange haze emanates from it. Nobody moves or tries to say anything until _____ snaps on a pair of gloves and takes _____ first step towards it. _____ shouts in my ear:

"We shall by mornin' inherit the earth. Our foot's in the door."

Dennis Tafoya

Dennis Tafoya lives near Philadelphia and is the author of three crime novels set in and around the city. His short stories have appeared in magazines and anthologies such as *Philadelphia Noir* and *Best American Mystery Stories*. His work has been nominated for multiple awards and been optioned for film and television.

Vivian Days

ivian was marching and we were following. I don't know where mother and father were. Wherever mothers and fathers went during the long days. Vivian watched us, but not like the other nannies or babysitters on Cherry Street, watching the kids playing in the yard while they smoked and gossiped. Vivian didn't gossip. On Vivian days we would go places, to the zoo or the lake, or she bundled us all up, Mason and me and even the baby and we rode the North Shore line into Chicago. She marched, truly, lifting her green boots high and swinging her arms as we tried to keep up. Her too-big overcoat flapping from her shoulders, stalking the people on Sherman Avenue and taking pictures with the boxy camera that swung at the end of the strap around her neck.

Vivian days were snooping, watching, waiting for her to get a picture while the baby cooed and gurgled and Mason made a game of jumping from the curb or climbing in and out of junked boxes behind the Marshall Fields in Evanston. Vivian took pictures of women getting out of cars looking chic and old men sleeping on benches by the Michigan Avenue Bridge. She took pictures of trash sitting in bins and the police arresting people. Before mother put a stop to it, we would go down to Western Avenue in Roseland and Morgan Park and Vivian would take pictures of the men drinking from bottles wrapped in paper, sitting in chairs like you'd see in a nice living room only it was a vacant lot and the men were bums. And children, always. Fighting, crying, playing sweetly. Dressed up for church or just dirty and squatting on the curb, the boys in short pants and the girls in dresses and bows in their hair. Sometimes, she'd take a picture of nothing, just a glass door to an empty shop and it was only when she walked away and I could stand where she had stood that I realized she was taking her own picture, a reflection in the glass of her own sad eyes, the long face that sloped down to her vanishing chin. We would never (ever) get to see the pictures, but I could tell from the look on her face when she got something she liked. It was a kind of smile that said she *knew* something, and that knowing was good enough for her.

Sometimes she had a beret on her head, my favorite, but other times it was like the fedora my dad used to wear on Sundays for church. My brother Mason, smart but mean, said she looked like a nut, but I thought she looked like *Sally Baxter, Girl Reporter.* A little, anyway, like the way Sally looked on the cover of *The Lost Ballerina* or *Secret Island,* like a no-nonsense type but with maybe a little bit of glamor. If you see her from the right angle, I said to Mason. He said, *what angle, like from outer space?* My dad would sit in the open door of the Chrysler smoking a last cigarette before he headed to work and shaking his head at my mother. He said under his breath *who is she, Willie and Joe in that getup?* I didn't know who that was, but my brother gave me that know-it-all look and said he means Vivian looks like an army man. Later when everything went wrong and my parents made Vivian go, I stayed up late with mother and we watched Casablanca and when Ingrid Bergman went into Claude Rains' office and she was wearing a white hat like a wide bowl over her head and had a serious look because she knew no matter how charming Claude Rains was that he couldn't be trusted and there was terrible danger everywhere. I thought with her face serious and holding back her fear, trying to make herself look empty and invulnerable, that Ingrid Bergman looked *exactly* like Vivian. I didn't say anything, but I had to put one hand over my eye and squint to keep from crying.

***

It all went wrong because a woman died, a woman and her baby. It was nobody we knew, just a story in the newspaper, mother said. Vivian was taking us to the park and there was a newspaper in the *Sun-Times* box on Hibbard Road and Vivian stopped and took a picture of the box and the article. She liked to kneel and snap pictures of the newspaper headlines in the box. There had been other murders that summer, and Vivian collected the papers and read the articles. *Police Hunt Girl's Slayer* was one, and *Probe Slaying of Suburb Girl*. With the suburb girl herself, the photo blurry but you could see she was pretty, with a wide, white smile and freckles, maybe, though it might just have been the dots the newspaper used to make up the picture. This one was *Mother, Baby Found Slain*, and Vivian shook her head and leaned close to the box, leaning in with her long, fox-like nose and her short hair. Not stylish, not a shag like you'd see Jane Fonda on TV or like Mia Farrow with her Vidal Sassoon haircut in Life magazine, but flat and all-anyhow, like the boys in my grade at Sacred Heart.

Vivian bought the newspaper, counting through her nickels and dimes from the pockets of her big coat and stood reading phrases aloud. The first line was about the beaten and naked bodies. Vivian's mouth hung open and she looked around with a searching expression as if for someone to talk to about it. She read some of the words out loud, *church parking lot,* and *autopsy,* and *electrical cord.* She made a noise in her throat and wrapped the newspaper up tight and took it home. When mother came home Vivian locked herself in her room behind the white door at the top of the house. You weren't allowed in her room (ever) but I would sit outside quietly sometimes, holding my breath and that night I could hear her in there, paging through her newspapers, the pages fluttering and flapping and occasionally she would say something in her strange accent that my father said was a put-on but that I loved to hear because it made her different, even somehow changed the way she looked to me. The shape of her mouth, her lips pursed to fit the curling syllables. I told my mother it wasn't a put-on, that she spoke French to our baby brother and had taught him to say "hot" and "cold," and other things when she was feeding him and getting him dressed. That night I got into my pajamas and crept quietly down the carpeted hall, and through the door I could hear her say "police," and "strangled" and finally, "sex maniac." After that it was quiet except for the rustling pages and the snap of the shutter.

The next day Mother was going to meet grandmother and Vivian had us all up early so Mason and I could get on the train. She had the movie camera, which was called a Filmo and had a grip like a gun, along with the boxy one that hung around her neck. At Clybourn we had to change trains and Vivian took a picture of a beautiful woman with a hat that was like a scarf knotted at the top of her forehead. And she took pictures on the train, too, of men sleeping in the hard winter light, their mouths hanging, while my brother sneered and made click, click, noises and whirled his finger around by the side of his head in the international sign of someone is crazy, pointing behind her back in case I didn't know who he meant. I asked Vivian why the sleeping man had yellow fingertips and she said that was what happened when you smoked too much. Vivian went through her purse and sorted newspaper articles and maps and a train schedule. I took one of the articles from the pile on the seat next to her and read it, about the woman who had posted a notice on a bulletin board to babysit and gotten picked up by a stranger, her and her baby both. I read a few paragraphs and had to stop. There was a little map printed in the newspaper with squares labeled *VICTIM'S HOME* and *BODIES FOUND HERE.*

We got off at the Jefferson Park station and transferred to the Milwaukee Avenue Bus. Vivian stared hard at each man we saw, as if sizing him up as a killer of women and children. My throat began to close up, but we were only on the bus for a few minutes and I was grateful to get off and walk, even if it had clouded over and begun to get colder. Mason was making a show of how bored he was, kicking at the telephone poles, so Vivian yanked at his collar and stood him up straight. She looked like she wanted to give him a good smack (which father would have) and I thought that might be the end of whatever adventure we were on, but after a minute of staring at him, Vivian gave him the map and showed him an 'X' she had made in jagged pencil lines and said he could be the navigator.

He began sprinting ahead, pointing left or right, and Vivian marched (for real, like a soldier, swinging her arms), and I ran to keep up with her clomping feet and was out of breath.

At the X on the map we stopped, but there was nothing to see. It was a nice-enough neighborhood, not like Winnetka near the lake, with the big houses and wraparound porches, but buildings of small apartments with neat lawns. I said, "Who lives here?" and Vivian said, *the people who work for a living. The people who ride the bus.* She got the Filmo out, then, and began pointing it at the building across the street, the camera making a whirring noise. There was a man in a house across the street and she leaned in, twirling the ring on the lens. She saw me staring and handed me the camera and showed me how to move the dial so that I could see what she was seeing, a man talking on the phone and looking at us out the window. When I spun the dial he jumped toward me so that I had to take my eye away and make sure he was still safely in his room and not looming over us on Meade Street. Vivian said, this was where the woman lived. The woman who had been murdered.

She bent to the map with Mason and showed him where we were headed next while I shivered and looked up and down the street. I was wearing a pea coat from the Army Navy on Lincoln Avenue, which I had somehow persuaded mother to allow me to buy with my allowance and that I had adorned with a peace sign that I stitched on myself. My father sighed whenever he saw me wearing it, saying *Diane, you're not letting her wear that thing to school, are you?* and *bad enough I got General de Gaulle sleeping in my attic, now this one's dressing like a Wells Street hippie.* Mason ran on down Meade and Vivian clanked away after him so I scurried after, keeping to her flapping shadow and peering behind me into the blank windows and the alleys that faded into darkness behind the blocky apartment houses.

We came out on Milwaukee at a Jewel Market, where there were older women in cloth coats and knit caps and young women with little kids hanging out of shopping carts. It was nice to be around people and I felt some of the tension go out of my shoulders and neck. Vivian pointed the Filmo around again, stood in front of a bulletin board and read the little cards there. She put the camera down and went into her huge bag and came out with a tape recorder, holding the little microphone out with its curling gray wire. Mason said, *oh, god!* under his breath.

"Excuse me," Vivian said, hemming in a short woman with white hair against the wall near door. "Did you know the woman who was murdered?"

The woman's eyes were startled, bright, like the eyes of some small woodland animal. She had on a blue knit cap and reminded me of Mrs. Kaduc who came to clean our house. "Oh, the murder!" she said, "My girlfriend Alice knew her! Such a beautiful young woman."

"Did you know that she put an ad here? At the bulletin board? That's how he got her."

"Oh, I didn't know," the woman said, her lips drawn in. "That's a terrible thing. Is this for the news?"

Vivian pressed closer. "Her body was dumped at the church in Mt. Prospect. She and her baby. Do the people of the neighborhood talk about it? Are there theories about the man? If he might be some kind of maniac from the neighborhood?"

The woman was terrified now, her eyes going back and forth between Vivian's tape recorder and the bulletin board with its scrawled invitations to murder and violation. The woman said, "No! I don't know anything about that," and disappeared into the store as if into a burrow. Vivian tapped the microphone, unsatisfied.

Mason flapped the pages of the map. "Where to?"

We got back on the bus and got off to a crowd. There were people milling in front of a low building across the street and a hearse parked in front. A funeral home. We were across the street from the crowded parking lot, people getting out of their cars.

I said, "We're not going over there, are we?"

Vivian took the movie camera away from her eye and looked at me.

I could tell she wanted to. She went back to filming and while she worked, she said, "A woman is always alone in the world." She said it quietly, just to me. It finally had the thought that struck me like a physical thing, a sensation of warmth in the back of my head that this woman, the woman who had put herself in a position to be picked up by a stranger and taken away to her terrible death, that she was a nanny, like Vivian. That like Vivian she went out among strangers and took care of their children and that there was nothing that protected her except her own wits. Her physical presence, the way she dressed, the natural armor of her strangeness.

***

A few steps away was a place that sold religious things. The sign said, Church Supplies and Sacred Vessel Restoration. I said to Mason, "What are church supplies?"

He shrugged. "I guess all the candles and stuff." I went over to look in the front window and there were white robes like priests wore, and displays of books. Crosses on stands. Some normal stuff, too, I guessed. Christmas tree ornaments and things like that.

A man came out of the store and looked at me. He seemed weird, his hair swept away from a high forehead and his ears too long. He said, "Are you here for the funeral?"

"We're just taking a trip," I said. "For the day." I took a step closer to where Vivian stood at the corner. He followed. He watched Vivian filming.

"She was a Presbyterian," he said.

Vivian took the camera away from her eye and looked at him. "What was that?"

He said, "The woman. The woman and her daughter. They were left at the Presbyterian church."

I watched her size him up. She looked at his shoes, which were worn on the tops. His tie was crooked. The tips of his fingers were yellow. I whispered to Vivian, "He's a smoker."

She asked the man, "Are you a Presbyterian? Did you know her?"

"I don't understand that church," he said. "I became a Lutheran at Menard. The chaplain was a Lutheran. He said Jesus died for everybody, but the Presbyterians think it was just for the chosen. How could you live like that? Not knowing whether Jesus is for you?" He put his yellow thumb in his mouth and bit the nail. "I need Jesus on my side, no matter what I done." He lifted one elbow to point back at the religious store. "I sell bibles now." He tried to see into Vivian's bag. He asked, "Are you doing..." His voice trailed off. "What are you doing?"

Vivian took my hand in her cold fingers. "We're investigating," she said.

"Huh," said the man. "Like the police?"

"Anyone can investigate," she said.

Mason had come to stand by us. Out of the side of his mouth he said to me, "Did he say Menard?"

I tried to make my voice quiet, like his, smothering it with a breathy rasp. "What's Menard?"

"Prison."

Just then the bus came, hissing at the curb, and Vivian moved us over and we got on. The man watched us, then got keys out of his pocket and stood by a black Falcon like my uncle Frank drove, but this one had rusted-out fenders and dents in the doors.

When we got on the bus I watched the people coming and going across the street. I noticed for the first time a dog, a big, amiable-looking German Shepherd. It was standing on the roof of the funeral home, its tongue lolling, just happy to see people. Not knowing anything about the world.

***

Back in Winnetka we walked along Elm toward our house by the lake. The sun had come out, but it would be dark soon. At the corner of Maple where the park starts, Mason saw two of his friends by the water fountain and yelled to them and they waved him over across the street and he started out, not looking. Vivian grabbed at his elbow but he yanked away and walked off the curb and a car that none of us saw stopped short, Mason bouncing off the front bumper and smacking down hard onto the street. Vivian shook her head and said something in French (maybe) and knelt by Mason, who was stunned and blinking. There were families coming out of houses, and somebody yelled that from a front porch that they had called an ambulance and one of Mason's friends, Donny Ciprietti, ran down Maple and waved over a Winnetka police car. A woman came out of her house with a blanket and put it under Mason's head. He didn't seem hurt, just dazed and blinking.

There was a crowd now, women and children from the houses, some of whom I knew, and people talked excitedly and asked questions. As the police got out of their cars I realized no one had gotten out of the car that had hit Mason and then I saw it was a black Falcon with rust on the bumpers. The man from the store was sitting in the driver's seat smoking a cigarette. The police were asking questions and I tried to answer but Vivian, who should have been the one to explain was standing at the curb taking pictures. I tried to talk to her, telling her we should tell everything about the woman and her baby and the investigation and the man with yellow fingers, but she was clicking away, looking down into the camera, tilting her head to get the best angles on the car, Mason in the street holding his head, the big policemen with their hands on their hips. I was starting to cry a little, pointing out the man in the car to one of the police while he said, 'huh, is that right?' and lifting a hand to get his partner's attention when there was a yelp at the corner of the crowd and my mother appeared.

***

That was it for mother and father, that day. Not just Mason getting hit but all of it, the stacking of old newspapers in her room, eating cold peas from the can, her way of being that my father couldn't understand and seemed (to him) prickly and sour. It didn't help that at dinner after our day in the city the baby dropped his spoon and when my father picked it up and put it back on his tray, our little brother clapped his hands and said, "*Et voilà.*"

The following Monday Vivian was standing at the curb waiting for a cab, all her things stacked around her in piles, her boxes and bags and yellow suitcases. She was taking a picture, but I couldn't make out what she was photographing, what there was to see there on the lawn. I went to stand by her and touched her long gray coat, just her coat, because you didn't touch Vivian (ever), not to hold her, not to get a hug, and anyway she wasn't looking at me, she was hunched over the camera with ROLLEIFLEX in silver over the two lenses and looking down at the grass and the bright dandelions and buttercups and the long morning shadows of the elms. I handed her an article I had cut out from the Tribune about the bible salesman, who had confessed to the police. She took the article and folded it and put it in her purse.

The cabbie came and got out of his cab and whistled at the piles of boxes and bags and he asked what was the name and she said, "Call me Smith," and absently gave my collar a tug and smoothed the front of my dress, just a small move with her hand that wasn't much (but a lot if you were Vivian) then she supervised the man as he loaded everything, the springs of the cab creaking under the weight of all the junk. When he was almost done, lifting and replacing her battered metal trunk, trying to make it fit, she knelt on the grass and opened a green footlocker that was like something a soldier would have. Inside was a shelf of cameras, each carefully arranged, some wrapped in soft brown velveteen. She gave a small exhalation, a small grunt of consideration, touching the dull silver and scuffed black cases, an Exakta, a Leica, and finally she lifted one and unwrapped it and handed it to me. I looked at her and said something I don't remember anymore, a question, but she got into the cab and in a minute was gone down toward the lake. I stood where she had stood, holding the Rolleiflex and looking at the flowers on the lawn. I couldn't see anything, but it was Vivian and I knew, I knew it was something. She was looking for *something*.

It was only much later in a gallery in New York that I saw the picture she took that day. Between a photo of the beautiful young woman waiting for the train and a young boy riding a dark bay horse under the El, I saw it, recognizing instantly the brilliant summer lawn. Even without the rest of it, the corner of the old house by the lake or my father's Chrysler in the driveway or any of it, I knew that fragment of the place I'd grown up and I saw what she had focused the camera on. Her own shadow cast onto the grass, long arms jutting, the angular silhouette of the camera held to her shoulder, the tilted hat. The dark green shape of Vivian herself, dotted with bright flowers like stars.

Nora Thurkle

Nora Thurkle is from Catford, south-east London, and studied Creative Writing with the Open University. She placed second in the *London Magazine* Short Story Prize 2021 and was shortlisted for the 2021 Galley Beggar Press Short Story Prize for her story *Inaudible Frequencies*. She has also had work featured on *Lunate, Liars' League, Dear Damsels* and *The Toast*. Nora works as a primary school teacher.

The Things We Did
and Didn't Do

A *black line drawing on blue-lined paper, the edge frayed where it has been ripped out of a spiral-bound notebook. Four scratchy figures behind the scratchy rectangle of a school table.* Rose drew the picture of them during a History lesson. Ms Bailey had left them to it at the back of the class and Hayley watched Rose drawing, the flex and rise of tendons in her hands like the strings inside a piano. Rose's head was propped on her other hand, her chin resting in the V of thumb and forefinger, momentarily gazing off for inspiration. Hayley could smell her perfume – real perfume, not Impulse body spray like the rest of them wore.

Rose labelled the four of them in her thin scratchy handwriting, borrowing Daisy's pen because her own had begun to run dry and elbowing her when she tried to sneak a look before Rose was finished. The labels were unnecessary – each of the four figures was instantly recognisable. She added speech bubbles too.

The in-jokes in the speech bubbles are so unbearably moment-specific that it hurts, now, to read them. The page is slightly yellow.

Hayley thinks about when she used to look at her mother's old photos and papers, how ancient they looked. She had imagined she would never own anything that old.

Mr Franklin took over History halfway through year 10 and they couldn't get away with it anymore, the drawing and sending notes. He would come and perch on the desk, a yawn of hairy ankle and wrinkled sock between his shoes and the hems of his trousers. He told them stories about his last school, how rough it was and how a kid stabbed another kid in the bum during one of his lessons, playing it for laughs. Rose laughed and bantered with him. Daisy and Lily too. (He made fun of them, their little group, Lily and Rose and Daisy and… *Hayley*, like no one had ever pointed that out before, and they all laughed at that too.)

An overexposed photo of four teenage girls, an unmemorable high street behind them and the linear frame of a bus stop. They are climbing on each other, laughing, holding plastic shopping bags.

They slept over at Rose's house, which had so many rooms that some of them weren't even being used. When they had sleepovers they sometimes wouldn't encounter another person all night. At home, Hayley couldn't do anything without someone hearing her; she was always tense, her body a defensive curve, ready to turn and shoulder a door closed, to hide herself.

They mixed vodka with coke and added marshmallows because Daisy had seen it online. The marshmallows went heavy and soggy and everyone ended up spitting them into the bin, except Daisy, determined. They all bundled together onto Rose's bed to watch TV, the room slightly unsteady around Hayley. She leant on Rose's shoulder; Rose put her arm around her. From under her arm rose a tang of sweat, shockingly intimate, no trace of perfume. Hayley wanted to put her tongue on Rose's skin. She went to the bathroom and plunged her face into cold water, vomited into the toilet, brushed her teeth, felt better.

A folded sheet of cartridge paper, fingerprinted at the edges with black dust. Unfolded, a vortex of a face, lined and lined and lined in charcoal, as though it is exploding outwards. A white point at the centre where the face might begin again; the paper here is flaking, eraser-worn.

Rose had a free period after lunch on Fridays, some timetable quirk, and they found her already in the classroom when the rest of them turned up for History. Mr Franklin had his back turned, sorting through something in the cupboard. Rose was sitting in her seat already, looking at her textbook, doodling thorny vines. Her cheeks were pink.

Some of the younger girls had worked out which car was his and would hang around at the end of the day, asking him what he was doing that night, did he have kids, was he married. He was young enough to be spotted in the same pubs as some of their older siblings. He had danced with Lily's sister and her mates at Cube Bar at the weekend and been designated a laugh. Rose was always in his classroom these days; she said he gave good advice. They all knew she needed advice about something; she had been coming to school with raw red patches around her nostrils and shadows under her eyes and refused to talk about it.

Rose and Hayley took art while Daisy and Lily had technology. Rose had been working on a self-portrait in charcoal. It was glorious, an extension of the spindly, delicate style she used in her doodles of them, the ones she would rip out of her notebooks and pass under the table while teachers were distracted. She had used a rubber to lift out white highlights in her eyes, on her chin and the side of her nose.

One morning, before lunch, Rose destroyed her self-portrait, the charcoal sticks snapping into tiny pieces, her fingertips forcing them into the paper in severe, jagged lines. The teacher was talking to her in an undertone but she did not stop, black slashing again and again across the page, obliterating the drawing. Her face, looking at it, seemed blank; then Hayley saw the smirk at the corners of the mouth. She understood that Rose was acting out what was expected of her, and that just because she wanted to laugh did not mean that she thought it was funny.

Finally Rose put down the charcoal and asked Hayley for her rubber. The lesson ended minutes later and as she left the room, Rose dropped the picture into the bin without looking. Hayley went back to get it and slipped it between papers in her own folder. Because it was evidence of something, a testimony. Or because it revealed something private and guarded about Rose which Hayley could not resist taking for herself.

The next week, after school, Hayley went to speak to Mr Franklin when she knew that Rose had left early for an appointment. She walked past the box of programmes for the school production – Mr Franklin was co-directing – that was propping open the door.

She knew she didn't want advice from him, while being uncertain exactly what it was that she did want. She knew this brittleness that had grown on Rose recently like an exoskeleton had something to do with him. But she didn't want to mention Rose's name in that room – to conjure an image, the comparison unflattering to Hayley – to feel her friend looking over her shoulder, her face wearing the same placid expression as when they first met, aged eleven – to betray Rose by revealing her as just a teenager with issues as banal as the rest of them, like presenting him with a naked photograph of her – and although she was faintly aware that she wanted to provoke him and the situation, to make *something* happen, she could not go straight to it. And something about it was wrong, but she had to probe it, like tonguing a rotting tooth. She asked something stupid about homework.

He was standing on a chair, sticking something on the wall, and he got down and sat across from her, leaning forward like he was really listening. He made a stupid joke and a silence began to unfurl between them. She didn't know what to do in a silence like that, she felt it would drown her, so she cut it off by laughing. It was easy to laugh with someone when you knew they wanted you to laugh. She put a hand to her hair, remembering she hadn't brushed it since the morning, thinking about Rose's hair, smooth and sun-lightened. He got up and kicked the box of programmes to one side and closed the door.

He kissed her, and she knew she was supposed to want it, to be so grateful that she was receiving this blessing. She certainly didn't push him away, this older man, this handsome man that everyone wanted. She wanted to laugh, a breathlessness in her chest suddenly, and she thought about the screech of charcoal on paper. He was holding her upper arms and pulling. Not hard enough that anyone could call it violence. She felt the carpet on her knees, wiry and abrasive, and heard the chair thunk to the ground behind her, the noise dulled by the carpet, and smelled aftershave and sweat and coffee. She went still like a doll. A knee between her thighs, insistent. An unshaven chin and a hand holding her wrist up against the chair, a thumb pressing an ache into it. His solid body beneath the ironed cotton of his shirt.

She felt like she might have made up these details. But not the incredulous feeling, surely this wouldn't really happen, surely not her, she wanted to laugh again, her breath gone, it wasn't going to happen like this.

There were footsteps in the corridor and time began to pass normally again; his grip faltered and his weight shifted and she squirmed up and away, turning the door handle the wrong way at first before it took, and half-fell out of the classroom door, into air that smelled of school dinners and photocopy toner, and no one was there and she did not look behind her.

A yearbook, cheaply produced with interlocking blue shapes on the cover, text in swallowtail banners to suggest academic success, the school crest embossed to suggest tradition. The last few pages are a collage of photos from an end-of-year party; one shows four young women wearing shiny dresses, their faces sheened with makeup. Flowers pinned in hair, bare legs taut in high shoes, scarred forearms uncovered, a scorch of sunburn across nose and cheeks.

The sixth-form end of term party was the last time they were all together. Rose and Daisy had been sniping at each other for months. It was a relief, really, for the structure of school to fall away and release them from obligation.

Hayley went to visit Rose after she left for uni. She had cut her hair and stopped wearing so much makeup. She looked older; she looked beautiful. In a noisy pub full of backpackers, they downed shots and danced and hugged. On the way home, they stopped under the railway bridge so Rose could light a cigarette.

Hayley saw her right hand pinning Rose's left above her head against the bridge, felt the brick grazing their knuckles, tasted tequila on Rose's tongue, felt the slip of Rose's thighs in their opaque tights under her hand, her silver rings snagging on the nylon. She felt Rose pushing her away, saw Rose's tears, felt an undoing – how can you possibly, possibly know what someone wants?

Rose was looking at her oddly in the orange streetlight glow. 'You

OK?'

They shared the cigarette walking back and Hayley slept on the floor, her head on Rose's spare pillow.

It was easier just to close down her relationship with Rose and put it away. In a box, inside a cupboard. When she packed up all the drawings and photos – all the paraphernalia of friendship – she felt stupid somehow, trite, obvious. It had the same energy as a frustrated writer in a film screwing up a ball of paper and tossing it at an overflowing bin. She thought of Rose destroying that self-portrait, her deliberate, resigned actions posing as a loss of control.

Every dream takes place in her childhood home. The walls are in the wrong places sometimes, ceilings missing or lower than they were in reality, toilets and showers standing free in the kitchen or the little room she shared with her brothers. Rose is there, which she never was in real life. Hayley didn't have people over. Rose is there, in Hayley's sagging single bed with her grubby teddies, waiting for her. Her lips are soft, she smells of perfume. Hayley presses her body against Rose and wakes up pressing into her pillow.

A programme for a school musical production, a teenage girl made up and hairsprayed on the front, singing and looking away to the side, apparently candid. Tucked inside the programme, a photograph – a group of girls and a male teacher, the co-director, with his arms around the two on either side of him, expansive, smiling, his eyes emptied by the camera flash.

She hears that he's dead from Lily. Lily messages her a few times a year and they meet up with Daisy and swap surface news in some chain restaurant with inoffensive art on the walls and lots of chrome in the bathrooms. After Lily tells her about Mr Franklin she goes to the toilet and googles him on her phone, but she can't get WiFi. When she gets back to the table they are still talking about him. 'He was such a good teacher,' says Lily. 'And so young! It's unbelievable.'

'Yeah. Weird,' says Daisy. 'Do they know what he died of?'

'Didn't say,' says Lily. 'Didn't say anything about a long illness, whatever you usually get when it's cancer or something.'

'It's a shame,' says Hayley. She pauses carefully. 'To be honest I always thought he was a bit inappropriate. The stuff he told us. Joked about. You know?'

'You wouldn't get away with that now,' says Daisy.

'It was just banter,' says Lily.

'Was it, though?' says Daisy.

Daisy was the only one that Mr Franklin's charm couldn't touch. She already knew herself even then. More than that, she knew about men. Still, today, she doesn't let them lock in. She siphons off all the adventures she can and then she moves onto the next one.

Hayley looks at Daisy. Their eyes meet and Hayley breaks the connection, quickly, still not willing to be seen.

When she successfully googles him later, she finds a news article with a photograph at the top that is clearly taken from a social media profile. A man with a heavy jaw, lines around his mouth as he smiles. The photo has been cropped but there is still a hand resting on the man's arm, a shadow of dark hair in the corner of the frame. It says his death is 'not being treated as suspicious.' Another result further down the page refers to a 'leave of absence' from his work.

That evening Hayley takes out the box and starts to unpack the things inside. Scrap books and photograph albums. She is not sure why; she feels certain that she already knows everything they have to say.

Ellen Wiese

Ellen Wiese is a Chicago-based writer and theater artist currently working in Norwich. Her fiction has appeared in *Wigleaf*, *The Bookends Review*, and *Lost Balloon*, from which she received a 2020 Best Microfiction nomination, and her short story, *Noise*, was listed on *Glimmer Train's* 2018 Very Short Fiction Top 25. She has also developed short and full-length plays with Trap Door Theatre and Chimera Ensemble. Ellen is currently enrolled in the MA Prose Fiction program at the University of East Anglia.

The Walking King

Nested like the yolk in an egg, wick in a lamp, ball in a dog's mouth was a house with four windows. The east and west windows were for seeing the sun rise and come down again; through the north window they kept a lookout for the winter winds.

The house had three beds, two bodies, and one door. "What if the north wind gets inside the house and we can't get out?" asked Leïd. Gerde only shook her head. She had been born farther north than this, miles and miles farther north. In Gerde's North the wind blew snow drifts sixteen feet high against the front door. Men wore wide snowshoes to beat tracks from one house to another and you could make hard candy by throwing boiling syrup onto the snow.

On the wall next to the east window was a picture of the king. It gave the whole house a lopsided feeling: you couldn't help but look at it when you came in. "Who's that?" a traveler would ask. Leïd would look at Gerde. "That's the king," Gerde would say.

The king had a short-cropped beard and brilliant eyes. The kind of eyes that would say, "Fortune favors the persistent." "What's done is done." "There's more in heaven and on earth, Horatio." His nose was a little too long and pinched at the end.

The photo of the king was water-damaged: stained rivulets discolored the top of the picture and striped the top of his head in dark gray lines.

"Lovely house," the traveler would say.

"Thanks much," Gerde would say, or, "Better than a hole in the ground," if she'd had a few.

It *was* a lovely house, in Leïd's opinion. You could see everything there was to see about it by standing in one spot and turning in a circle.

Things weren't like that outside the house. Depending on the spot you stood, everything changed places: the light, the time of day, the creatures and the trees. You could plant your feet and turn in a circle and by the time you were facing the same way again everything would have shifted.

The forest had two landmarks: their four-windowed house and the river. "There never used to be a path here," Gerde would say as they walked the dirt track between the two. "That king wore ditches in the ground, walking back and forth."

Red lichen grew underwater on the river's banks and reached towards the current like a drowned woman. If they didn't keep their laundry away from the shore it would stain their things deep rusty brown.

Leïd had what Gerde said was "a thing about rivers." On laundry days she stared into the water and thought about all that water going past that she would never see again, all that new water rushing in that she could never look at long enough, the whole span of downriver and upriver constantly moving and her just looking, doing nothing at all.

The traveler would have to stay for dinner: the sun was going down already and the closest town was at least a morning's walk away. Depending on the direction you went, you could find your way to many places, but none less than a morning's walk.

The traveler would be heading east to the sunrise towns of the coast or west to the mines and factories and families who manned them. Sometimes the traveler would be going north, and this was the only time Gerde would express an interest in their destination. "Where to?" she would say.

Some were going to a city divided into quarters by two rivers, where residents met on the bridges in the evenings and talked and drank and laughed as lights went by on the barges below. Others were headed to a forest of timber that was shrinking, a forest very different from this one, younger and louder and full of dangerous animals. In the winter it stood like an army of skeletons and the locals were engaged in a constant struggle to cut it all down.

The travelers always disappointed: they were never going quite to Gerde's North.

Their forest was old pine. It was quiet – that was something a traveler would always say. "It's so quiet here," they would say, and pull their coat around them. Or, "I bet you sleep well." And then toss and turn all night.

The forest swallowed sound: you walked out between the trees and sank into pine needles up to your ankles. It didn't want you to sing or whistle or talk as you walked (on this Gerde and the forest agreed). They used pine needles for tea and for starting the stove, and in exchange they didn't sing or whistle or talk when they passed under the trees. Only the river ignored this: it laughed like a crazy man through their sheets and buckets. That was another thing Leïd didn't like about rivers.

Maybe the traveler didn't want to stay. "I'm used to sleeping rough," they would insist. "I can't impose on your hospitality." Sometimes they looked sideways at Leïd, like there was something going on she couldn't understand. (Leïd did understand. If a traveler tried something while they were sleeping, Gerde hit them so hard with the fire poker that it left a permanent dent.) But Gerde always prevailed. This was one of her great gifts: she drew herself up and her face darkened, not in a way that promised immediate violence, but in a way that warned you it was in your best interest to listen. Her eyes looked down into yours and informed you that they'd seen a lot more than you had and if you wanted to *keep* seeing things you'd take her good advice. "We'll make up a cot," Gerde said, "I insist." And they would, on a pallet on the floor with spare quilts and pillows pulled from the chest at the end of her bed.

The traveler had come as far as they could to make it way out here. Gerde never asked why: Leïd sometimes did, when Gerde was outside. Gerde didn't like nosiness. "They aren't asking us what *we're* doing here," she'd tell Leïd. "Show them the same courtesy."

The traveler was going to visit family or looking for a job. They were fleeing something, seeking something, moving without thinking, insane (with fear or longing or exhaustion or vice). The travelers were lots of things, but thanks to Gerde they always stayed the night. Some travelers must not have made it to their house in the clearing in the middle of the woods. But Leïd never saw them (and neither, she thought, did anybody else, ever again).

Night came down more quickly in the forest than anyone expected, even Leïd who had spent her whole life here. You tried to time out dusk and the sun went down an hour earlier for spite. That was the use of the west window: you could keep an eye on the sunset from a safe vantage point and make sure it didn't pull any tricks.

Leïd was a light sleeper. Usually this wasn't a problem: the quiet of the pine forest sunk deep down in the evening, seeping through the spaces between the roots of the trees and closing their front door for them. But sometimes she woke up in the middle of the night, heart pounding as if someone had yelled in her ear.

The dark room of their house would be as silent as ever. Slowly, something would grow brighter outside, illuminating the ceiling and her hands on the quilt. The bright yellow beam would crash through the window like a wave, rush from floor to ceiling in a moment, and disappear.

A traveler brought their own kind of noise into the house. If they didn't snore, they tossed and turned; if they didn't stir, they breathed too loudly. Sometimes Leïd thought she could hear them blinking in the darkness. If a traveler was staying, Leïd would be up. And, sometimes, the traveler would be too. They were a long ways out from everything, and many people slept like they were dead (they weren't, usually, and if they were Gerde brought them to the river with the laundry). But sometimes a traveler would be sleepless anyway.

"Are you awake?" Leïd would say. That was another of Gerde's great strengths – she could sleep through anything. The traveler would jump and Leïd would see their eyes reflecting the light through the windows.

"Yes," they would say, or, "Sorry," or pretend to be asleep. Leïd would get out of bed and walk to the south window. This was its only use.

They would eventually join her and the two of them would look out, Leïd and the traveler who was tall and pockmarked, lithe with long hair in a black braid, stocky with laughlines spreading from their eyes like roots. Since the sun had gone down everything had switched places. The trees stood in their shadows.

"My grandmother told me stories," one traveler said. "In the middle of the forest was a house with four windows, and in the house lived a woman and a girl…"

"How is your grandmother?" Leïd asked politely.

"She's passed," the traveler said, "Many years ago."

The trees leaned slightly as the wind pushed its way between them. As the forest steadied, something far away kept leaning, bending closer to the ground, and finally lifting out of the earth and rising past the house, past the canopy. Beyond it, another limb shifted and rose, higher and higher...

Leïd and the traveler followed that logic up and up and up, past the pointed tops of the pines. Ten points scraped the sky, impossibly large and impossibly far away. Yellow eyes gleamed with a light so bright it could be mistaken for the moon. Even higher were the stars, framed between the points of its antlers. Leïd knew this from every traveler: the stars above their house were like nowhere else in the world.

"What is that?" the traveler would say, or just stand there and shake.

"He's walking," Leïd would say. Through the trees, they could see the eyes sweep the landscape like searchlights, illuminating glimpses of the forest in the distance and then blinding them for a moment as its gaze swung past, even a thing as big as this walking in silence, muffled by the carpet of needles that covered the forest floor.

The restless traveler would leave in the morning. There had only been one traveler who had stayed, lured by the quiet under the branches.

The house with four windows was the still center of something, a place for passing through – it was dangerous to stay too long or wonder too deeply. Travelers sought their destination and didn't linger in the loam silence of the woods. The king who tried to listen between the trees, who walked paths through the pine needles into the ground below, searched still.

Gerde would tidy the room and gather the traveler's bed things into the sheet, pulling up the corners and knotting them. Her eyes would sweep the room for anything out of place and, if Leïd was watching closely, she would see them stutter on the unused center bed for just a moment.

While Gerde looked at the bed, Leïd looked at the water-damaged photo, looked and looked much longer than she would usually have been allowed to, looked until the echo of familiarity in the jaw and the set of the eyes brought a half-memory back to her body, a memory that would fade if she thought about it too hard, located somewhere between the lines of damp that striped the king's temples.

"Well, that's that," Gerde would say, gathering the bundle. "Laundry won't do itself." And they would make their way down to the river, Leïd lagging behind with their dishcloths and underwear and skirts, and the trees were in different places again.

Judges' Profiles

Tom Drake-Lee managed bookshops, was a sales representative for Bloomsbury and then Penguin Random House, before becoming sales director at Vintage for twelve years, where he worked with writers such as Margaret Atwood, Salman Rushdie, Toni Morrison, and Michael Ondaatje. Tom also helped establish the commercial success of writers including Ocean Vuong, Edmund De Waal, Helen Macdonald, and Ottessa Moshfegh. In 2021 Tom joined the DHH Literary Agency as an Associate Agent and is starting to build a client list across fiction and non-fiction.

Irenosen Okojie is a Nigerian-British author whose bold, experimental works create vivid narratives that play with form and language. Her debut novel *Butterfly Fish* and short story collections *Speak Gigantular* and *Nudibranch* have won and been shortlisted for multiple awards. Her work has been optioned for the screen. She is the co-presenter of the BBC's *Novels That Shaped Our World* podcast, *Turn Up for The Books*, alongside Simon Savidge and Bastille frontman Dan Smith, the follow up to the TV series. A fellow and Vice Chair of the Royal Society of Literature, Irenosen is the winner of the 2020 AKO Caine Prize for her story, *Grace Jones*. She was awarded an MBE For Services to Literature in 2021.

Jessica Taylor is the co-owner of Max Minerva's Bookshop independent bookshop in Bristol. She is also a Regional Sales Manager (South West) for Penguin Random House and was a *Bookseller* Rising Star in 2020. Previously, she helped develop collections for the Singapore National Library and ran an online bookstore in Australia.

Acknowledgements

We owe a huge thank you to the following people for their wonderful contributions to this year's Bristol Short Story Prize:

Firstly, to all the writers who entered our 2022 competition and who provided our readers and judges with such a wide-ranging, globe-spanning, era-travelling and enriching reading experience. We are extremely grateful for every single submission we received; thank you for sending your stories to us.

Enormous thanks also to: Martin Booth, Jo Borek, Harry Boucher, Andi Bullard, Joe Burt, Jo Darque, Tom Drake-Lee, Mark Furneval, Martyna Gradziel, Lu Hersey, Chris Hill, Sandra Hopkins, Jeanette Jarvie, Richard Jones, Amy Lehain, Lynn Love, Rosa Lovegood, Mike Manson, Bertel Martin, Catherine Mason, Louis Melia, Natasha Melia, Peter Morgan, Dave Oakley, Irenosen Okojie, Dawn Pomroy, Thomas Rasche, Pam Smallwood, Jess Taylor, Liz Tresidder, Jonathan Ward, Sol Wilkinson.

And finally, a massive thank you to you for buying this anthology. We hope you enjoy the stories as much as we have.

2022
Bristol Short Story
Prize Longlist

(Stories are listed A-Z by writer)

Manifesto – Nathan Bailey
Welcome to Otherhood – Yanjanani L. Banda
Cat Got Your Tongue – Leah Carter
Selkie – Sophie Develyn
Grey Unsilent Fragments – Angela Sangma Francis
Happy Ever After With Bear – Rosie Garland
Ghosts of the Wind River Valley – Paddy Gillies
Sunshine Beach – Lizzie Golds
Ruby Solitaire – Brad Gyori
Arranging Flowers – Josh Hallam
Sheriff's Calls – Claire Harman
Skin – Christopher Harrisson
Oranges – Jim Hilton
Place Your Returns on the Trolley to Your Left – Sam Horton
Desperate Things – Elleanna Jenkins
We Are Now Approaching Wellingborough – Helen Kennedy
Rivers – Sophia Khan

Lightning Girl – Elen Lewis
The Nudge – Anna Linstrum
Naanwai – Ananya Mahapatra
Unidentified Recurrent Incendiary Phenomenom – Oscar Martens
Ribs: Twig-Like – Charlotte McCormac
Girls and Boys – David Micklem
Salt Colonies - Shrutidhora P Mohor
Fray's Desk – Padraig Murphy
Becoming – Kate O'Grady
Once – Jyoti Patel
Whatever Happened to Maggie – Nigel Pettman
Red Tide – Nola Poirier
A Cure For All Our Ills – Diana Powell
Unknown Territory – Sara Probst
Wimmy Road Boyz – Sufiyaan Salam
Still Life With Lemon – Rachel Sloan
OldFish – Johanna Spiers
Coconut – Kailash Srinivasan
Elision – Henry Stennett
Vivian Days – Dennis Tafoya
The Things We Did and Didn't Do – Nora Thurkle
Finding Kevin – Fiona Ritchie Walker
The Walking King – Ellen Wiese

Winner of the 2022 Sansom Award for Bristol writers
OldFish – Johanna Spiers

Notable Contenders
(these stories were in the running for the longlist until the final decisions were made)
News from the Interior – Tammy Armstrong
The Bodhisattva's Gift – Emmeline Chang

Notable Contenders

Provenance of the van der Meer Pyxis by Anonymous (Abridged) –
Amanda Hildebrandt
American Hegemony – Phoebe Hurst
Lit and Left to Burn – Gaynor Jones
Drifting the White Line – James Martin Joyce
Mulier – Lauren Upton
Ivie's Room – Claudia Vulliamy